CONCERTO FOR SENTENCE

Concerto *for* Sentence

(AN EXPLORATION OF THE MUSICO-EROTIC)

EMILIYA DVORYANOVA

TRANSLATED FROM THE BULGARIAN
BY ELITZA KOTZEVA

DALKEY ARCHIVE PRESS

Originally published in Bulgarian as *Kontsert za izrechenie*
by Obsidian Publishers, Sofia, 2008

First edition, 2016

Library of Congress Cataloging-in-Publication Data
Names: Dvorëìanova, Emilièìa, author. | Kotzeva, Elitza, translator.
Title: Concerto for sentence : (an exploration of the musico-erotic) / Emilya Dvoryanova ; translated from the Bulgarian by Elitza Kotzeva.
Other titles: Konëtìsert za izrechenie. English
Description: Victoria, Texas : Dalkey Archive Press, 2016. | "Originally published in Bulgarian as Kontsert za izrechenie by Obsidian Publishers, Sofia, 2008" -- Verso title page.
Identifiers: LCCN 2015017082 | ISBN 9781628970777 (pbk. : alk. paper)
Subjects: LCSH: Violinists--Fiction. | Women musicians--Fiction. | Music in literature--Fiction. | GSAFD: Love stories.
Classification: LCC PG1038.14.V67 K6613 2015 | DDC 891.8/134--dc23
LC record available at http://lccn.loc.gov/2015017082

Partially funded by the Illinois Arts Council, a state agency.
This publication is supported in part by an award from the National Endowment for the Arts

This book was published with the support of the program
National Book Center at the National Palace of Culture.

Dalkey Archive Press
Victoria, TX / McLean / Dublin / London
www.dalkeyarchive.com

Dalkey Archive Press publications are, in part, made possible through the support of the University of Houston-Victoria and its programs in creative writing, publishing, and translation.

Cover: Art by Katherine O'Shea

Typesetting: Mikhail Iliatov

Printed on permanent / durable acid-free paper

CONCERTO FOR SENTENCE 1

. . . it must be an Amati, because the sound is engrossed in itself, muffled and inverted, carrying that strange patina the E chord never makes unless it's made on an Amati, otherwise this trill would have sounded silvery, instead it dives into opaque whiteness, like a cream-colored lace, as though played in D . . . but it could also be a Guarneri, especially if the softness of the A is leading me astray and is actually due to his magic fingers drawing out the tone so voluptuously, caressing the violin . . . it's so wonderful, it's divine . . . though if it had been a Guarneri, the sound would have sparkled in light blue . . . but because I was fifteen minutes late, I can't tell the make of the violin, he was furious, he didn't even answer my question, although he didn't seem to suspect anything . . . if he'd nursed even the least suspicion, I would have been able to see the reason for his rage and wouldn't have bothered to ask—Amati or Guarneri—moreover, it wasn't a good time for questions, the hall had fallen completely silent in expectation . . . the only noise in the auditorium was our squeaking steps when the sound sprung from the strings, and that motif uprooted me, it tore me out of myself, and then, when it spilled over into the lower register . . . it was as though the strings were inside me, the sound caressed me so tenderly, I've never experienced it before, and I'll tell him—I don't want it to

continue like this anymore, I can't take the roughness anymore, the coldness, the way he puts his hand on the closest seat adjacent to him so I have to cross to sit just where he wants me, and be sure not to touch him in the process, and now there's an awfully tall man looming over my chair and I can't see . . . I'll put up with it somehow, and when the concert is over I'll make a clean breast of things . . . I'd bet that it's an Amati, but then he'd ask me, How much do you bet?—and he'd make fun of me, and anyway where does he get the nerve—I asked him so gently, because you'd think, being married, we might also be friends: Amati or Guarneri? but he didn't deign to answer, squinting at me angrily, just because I was late, thanks to all that snow, everything is buried under the snow, but he doesn't suspect where I really came from, and we crawled so slowly in that car, there was zero visibility, snowflakes wove crazy blankets in the air, and the kettledrums were late by a fraction of a second, but the oboe salvaged the moment—as though nothing had gone wrong—and the car almost got stuck, everything was so slippery . . . did he even make it back home, did he make it back after he dropped me at the corner, and it's still snowing heavily, and I imagine how
I could have stayed there, at the foot of the mountain, how it would be snowed in together with him, I wouldn't even mind missing the concert in exchange for that, for an eternity by that fireplace, where the wood crackled and spurted sparkles like snowflakes on fire, I would let myself burn in those sparks, because his arms . . . and what amazing fingers this man has, look at how he

touches his violin, as if he's captured its soul—*âme* in French, *anima* in Italian, which words are also used to refer to a violin's sound post, that essential dowel inside the instrument, attaching top and bottom and vital to its resonance: a violin's anima is both spirit and structure—it's as if he's slipped inside it in such a way that you forget to think about his virtuosity (Amati? or Guarneri after all?)—I so hate when someone ignores me, but I won't allow it to ruin the concert for me, I only have to get rid of the unpleasant feeling of his sitting beside me radiating rage—even the music can't calm him down, he's radiating rage, he's a violinist too, he should feel the anima, he should melt, but I won't let it bother me and when the concert's over I'll tell him everything—confession is the best route, I should at least give him a reason for his rage, and after all he did try to get me here on time, to drop me off just a moment before the concert began, so that I wouldn't have any troubles, we couldn't even spare time for a last kiss . . . I just slammed the car door and ran . . . which is sad, without that kiss I feel as though I've sunk into an unexpected fermata, silence charged with sound, and I can't escape it, and here comes the theme, it always engrosses you in its sadness, and it's spilling out, he's spilling it over the brim of his instrument, he's raising the wave of the theme so high as to engulf the entire orchestra, absorbing it all into the sound of his violin, a sound seemingly opaque but capable of penetrating everything, as it pervaded me, I've never experienced anything like it, his hands are barely touching the strings, it seems effortless, unforced, like magic, sending out wave after wave . . . and the pizzicati pulled away, soaring, they climbed up to where the waves broke—which cadenzas will he play? . . . of course, his own cadenzas, and the music swells up once again, swells to the point of that tremolo, after which it manages to hang suspended, waiting for the phrase to follow, suspended for a moment timed by him to perfection before the phrase drags the orchestra up to its highest point yet, wrenching the music out from inside me, God, what a sense he has for the finale here, I'm shaking . . .—no, I've never felt so immersed in a single chord, in a culminating chord, there's nothing beyond it, only the andante . . . I'm happy now, hearing it, I'm happy and I will confess everything to him, I'll tell him that I'm in love with someone else now, that we'll have to separate, because I can't be apart from that someone else anymore, and I still carry his smell on my skin . . . now everything is melting around me, as if the air had frozen still for a moment and has now been released . . . and I can see his fingers quivering within the sound they're sustaining, barely touching the strings in a gentle vibrato . . . it's as if the note will resonate forever, though together with the clarinet it will soon lower itself into the deepest groan, but then the flute will come, I know, to wake it back up—God, it's so beautiful! why do I have to suffer, why can't I simply tell him how the logs cracked and groaned in the fireplace and how the fire scattered its light around us, its warm reflections embracing me body and soul . . . even now, when I think about it, I feel its heat running up and down my body—listen to that flageolet, no, not only that one, this whole series of flageolets lined up in the air, you could almost imagine they're strung together on an invisible thread—what kind of violin is this? what kind of hands?—Amati or Guarneri?—but it doesn't matter, I'll find out somehow, maybe it's even in the program, but I had no time to check, the lights were already out when we entered the hall, and everyone was waiting for the first note . . . no, I don't want it to be over, the kettledrums will soon announce the end with that fading tremolo, and the last trill will resound on the A and the E . . .—it must be an Amati, yet the A doesn't have quite the same timbre, so specific, which always soothes you and drags you down . . . maybe it's a Guarneri after all . . . I so much feel like crying because everything is over and the people are already raving, applauding ecstatically, but I wish I could take back the time, hear it again and again . . . I wonder what he'll play for an encore . . .

. . . encore . . . encore . . .

—Goodness, darling, it was unbelievable, inconceivable, no one's ever gotten under my skin like that . . . no, his performance didn't just move me, it shook me—have you ever seen gentler fingers? This is such a perfect, fairy-tale winter night, it's so romantic, I don't want to go right home—do you want to walk for a while? my mother doesn't mind staying with the kids . . . by the way, when we were going inside, you didn't answer my question about the violin, I even thought that you were mad at me, was I wrong? . . . well, Amati or Guarneri?

—*Maggini*, dear, *Maggini*, I was only trying to give you a chance to guess for yourself . . . you'll never learn, will you . . . you just lack the right ear, my dear . . .

—Well, after all, what matters is whether you enjoy it . . . the way it sounds . . .

CONCERTO FOR SENTENCE 2

. . . and here he is, in the flesh, my students' idol, they're all tempted by that unnatural perfection of his, he's clearly some sort of Don Juan

how can I convince them?

I can see at least five of them here enthralled by his beige shoes, beige suit . . . he looks like a clown and has no respect . . .

this world . . . this oblivious world . . . they applaud ecstatically . . .

. . . the first A of the first violinist, the first A . . . he responds:

a fourth,

a fifth . . .

a seventh . . . isn't the E slightly lower than it should be . . .

no, everything is precisely right, the sound is perfect, I've always thought that some Maggini are better than a Stradivarius, they give out different tone colors, the sounds are cinnabarine, bloody, it's amazing what one can tease out of a violin like this . . . I'd like so much to touch its scroll, its pegs . . . the neck is perfect, the fingerboard protrudes slightly, it's longer than they usually are . . . by as much as two centimeters . . . though they say the magic lies in the f-holes and the belly . . . —I'll die, and die incomplete, without ever having had a chance to even touch one of those darlings . . . there's only one here, but she keeps it hidden . . . and she doesn't even perform anymore, although she was good . . . very good . . . perhaps because of the violin . . . and while my students scrape along on some Cremonas, I always tell them—the violin, the violin, kids . . . its anima . . .

. . . he's about to begin, the beginning is the most important part, everything originates there, condensed in the first note . . . you can't make a mistake there . . . not in the first phrase, if you fail there, then . . . well, that's what I tell them . . .

. . . come on, lift your bow . . .

. . . he lifted his bow . . .

. . . damn it . . . it always happens like this . . . here come some real idiots, dilettantes, lifelong philistines, why do they have to show up now of all times . . . and the seats squeak in front of me and so at the very beginning I can't hear the most important . . . it's a man and a woman—she has a sweater on, pants, the world is really and resolutely going right to hell, how could you be late for something like this, how could you show up in a sweater, everyone had gone quiet, the crucial moment was about to arrive, and then, all of a sudden . . . squeaking . . . the seats opening and closing . . . people standing up to make way . . . no, they have no shame . . . ignorant people like this couldn't possibly know how important the first sound is, the first turning into the second, the merging of the phrases, even if you could only hear that one part, everything else would become clear—you could fly away—but the music has already fled and with it, its secrets—barbarians . . .

they finally take a seat, it's likely that they don't even realize what they've done, next to them are some young people whispering . . . scandalous . . . and I even know the guy who's doing it, a young violinist, a promising one, but whispering all the same . . . no, there's no hope, and after having waited for so long to hear this one little nuance, I missed it . . . now how long will he make the fermata . . . it's so difficult to be able to feel out the proper length . . .

he took a small pause, took a breadth . . . yes, the violin's singing, it's the instrument closest to the human voice, it breathes, and it breathes,

and the sweater woman in front of me is still shifting around in her seat even now, and he too is taking a moment to have a look around the hall, of course . . . it's not clear why people like *this* go to a concert at all, maybe just to see who else is attending, and then there's that sweater . . . how is such a lack of respect even possible, well, it's quite clear—it's just like his beige shoes, beige suit . . . they're doing it all on purpose . . .

no class whatsoever . . .

no class . . .

but the sound is magnificent; if you listen carefully, you can immediately tell the violin apart from others, the Maggini, that beauty, soars above everything else, it subjugates the rest of the orchestra, all the other instruments are on their knees . . . and it sounds like a brunette, you know, it's never occurred to me before, but a Guarneri, for instance, sounds like a blonde . . . or maybe not . . . gender is a tricky question, in this case . . . this violin is actually a man . . . anyway, it's masculine . . . or no? . . . an ambiguity . . . of sorts . . .

it glides into the notes, as if passing through them—that's worth some thought: where is the tone and where the violin, how do they merge, which one goes into the other . . . he didn't handle the slur very well; he barely even acknowledged it, simply repeated the same note, even though it's definitely on the score . . . younger players think they can just do what they like, I'm always having to remind them—fidelity, fidelity to the notes, kids, they are the alpha and the omega—I try to impress it on them, but they're all corrupted by jazz, they think everything is possible, they think they don't need any rules . . . no, I'm not being fair . . . now, this phrase . . . magical . . . it even sent shivers down the spine of the sweater woman in front of me, as though she actually had ears to hear, I saw it . . . the little sweater shivered . . . how is that possible? As if she weren't in a temple of art, but up in the mountains . . . she needs a fireplace and a bear skin . . . how can the man sitting next to her tolerate her vulgarity, or can't he tolerate it at all . . . no, these orchestras of ours will never learn . . . they'll always mess something up, the kettledrums shouldn't be pounding like that, they have to be a little muffled, and the trombone, I'd say, isn't living up to its reputation, it's dropping off right before the finale, right when the violin is getting ready for its supreme moment . . . exactly when all the instruments need to be perfect, so that the violin can enter in full force . . . and here it is, it storms into the prevailing calm . . .

Maggini

Maggini

Virginia . . . just another name, but how it unfolds, how it singles itself out, as though it's unique in the world . . . there's no instrument like her, now it'll show what it can do, all on its own, what it can do in the cadenzas, it will play itself, by itself, but using his hands . . .

and she comes in here wearing a sweater . . . that's why men are so hopeless today, poor bastards—there are simply no real women around anymore . . . he's already entered the cadenzas, actually he navigated them with something like brilliance, I have to hand it to him . . . although something is nagging at me . . . it's wrong, they're his own cadenzas, not what's in the score—the masters always write in their own particular cadenzas, but this one apparently thinks he's a master in his own right . . . no, no, this is wrong, it's just a bit excessive, it lacks the classic feel, it lacks moderation . . . but it seems that everyone else is entirely enraptured—it's the end of the world . . . only his technique is impeccable—I have to acknowledge that—his technique is impeccable, and just as in a magic trick, presto, the cluster of notes will vanish, like the wind it will rustle by, in the end the orchestra will chime timidly in, trying to match his approach. . . yes, here it is, it's just endorsing his errors, ingenuously confirming his arrogance . . . making the score to sound just as ingenuous, and now . . .

everything is confirmed.

Silence . . . for God's sake, don't you move . . . who's this idiot with the temerity to clap his hands now? God, how profane . . . and why are so many people coughing during the most important silence in the piece?

Più presto

and here comes the andante . . .

Andante . . . slower, go even slower . . . they're always speeding up the tempo, these days; they can't beat back the time, can't tame it, the time kills them, sweeps them away . . . take it more slowly, please . . .

it's beyond me, but now, in these phrases here, the Maggini has achieved perfection, what a perfect sound . . .

. . . a perfect ritual. Virginia prepares the music in herself, warms up the bath, her concert is to begin at two, from my office I can hear the water running

I added my own notes to the watery tones in the tub . . . —Dear, I'm going to take a bath, don't you peek . . . but I was playing music and imagining her . . . Maggini, dear, you're gorgeous, I know, your hair is dripping with . . . the second theme, absolutely perfect, in this concerto the secondary themes in all the movements are bound together by their uniform beauty, in fact they create the whole . . .

. . . if you were with me now, Virginia, you would be looking contemptuously at that little sweater, underneath which I can see the shoulder blades shiver, yes, I can see it, underneath it all she's a woman after all . . . but nonetheless, people today don't get it at all . . .

. . . will you rub lotion on my back, please, dear . . .

the softest skin, and her dress thrown on the bed—all this is because of the music and because of me . . .

classic, classic . . . Maggini, you could see how he must have been getting ready all day for this communion inside his instrument now, in the evening, as he moves into moment of moments . . . one needs such a careful touch here, the most difficult flageolets must be extracted . . .

. . . a little bit of pomade . . .

. . . make-up . . .

. . . a touch of lace, and Virginia, I'm looking at you, astonished, and we both know all this is for me . . . a kiss on the curve of your ear, on your collarbone, on your slender neck . . . and you would enter—lit in the brightest of spotlights, which will fade with the intro, and you will submerge into the music . . . so lovely, fragrant . . . and under the lace, your shoulder blades shiver . . . because you hear this . . . how it sinks away into . . . there it is,

con sordino

. . . perfect resonance . . .

there's no room for silence, no time . . .

Attaca

. . . well now. Applaud.

Encore.

Now what sort of encore will he play . . . something light? . . . no, he doesn't seem to go in for "light" . . .

I admit—he captivated me. But that's not the end of it. Sure, everyone's clapping—what do they know?

But there was really something off about that performance, something wasn't right, no . . . and now I have to delineate that wrongness for the students. If only Virginia could have been here, if only she had lived, not been taken from me so prematurely, I'd have told her about all of this and because she was so perfectly able to listen, simply listen, I'd have been able to explain . . . you need a perfect resonance . . .

The woman . . .

Encore.

CONCERTO FOR SENTENCE 3

Mind-boggling, mind-boggling, mind-boggling, I keep repeating it until I feel as though I'm going to faint, there must be some reason, a Freudian one, as they say, when a word impresses itself upon you and you don't know how to push it away, a virus in your consciousness, you keep repeating it, repeating it, I think I used it in the coffee shop before the concert, but the concert is mind-boggling too, mind-boggling even in advance, because it hasn't started yet, *he* hasn't come on stage yet, only the instruments in the orchestra are there, letting go a muffled blat waiting for the conductor, but it's mind-boggling that I'll now be able to listen to him live—you praise him too much—he told me—I don't praise him too much, I just like how he plays, although I know I don't know that much about it, at least not as much as you do—I don't know *any more* than you, and I don't like him at all, I'm just getting sick of everything, and, you know, if I get sick of music . . .—you'll get sick of life—that's right . . . and we ordered two pieces of Garash cake—I love Garash cake, but imagine if we could order Sachertorte—in Bulgaria one can't get Sachertorte, not the real thing, it only exists in Thomas Bernhard's books—but now even in Bulgaria we'll be able to hear this great master play, it's nothing less than mind-boggling, it's great that you could get us on the guest list, get us tickets, no matter that it was so last-minute that I barely had time to get dressed . . .

but I used the word in a different context and now I can't get rid of it, even when the conductor is already in front of his stand, that's the really mind-boggling thing, always at the beginning of a concert when the lights fade it seems like people fade for each other too, they respond each on his or her own to the raised baton as though they are themselves getting ready to play, but he hasn't even raised the baton yet, because *he* isn't here yet, he isn't here . . . but any moment now . . . I so want to hear something mind-boggling . . . to have my mind boggled with the taste of the cake, which isn't Sachertorte, unfortunately, he's told me so many times about Sachertorte since he came back—you know what, why don't we go to Vienna?—it's not impossible, but it's unlikely—and it would be mind-boggling to see St. Stephen's Cathedral, as indeed it's mind-boggling that he's now appeared on stage in a beige suit and beige shoes—this must be a concession to the image of the commercial, disheveled hipster violinist—no, it's not a concession to the commercial—he brings the young people in—not that we're not young too—but I'm not interested in his shoes or suit—I don't mind them, should we order a drink, it's terribly cold outside, it's snowing, and there's still another half an hour before the concert is supposed to begin . . .

here he is . . .

his hair is sticking right up too, and he has a mind-boggling callus, a violin hickey you might say, or do they call it fiddler's neck, no, it's huge, really mind-bogglingly big—I've never seen another violinist with a callus of that size . . . and my husband was stunned and looked at me—"That's a hell of a hickey!"—a big blotch, all red, and now he was adjusting the violin on the top of it . . . and A, A, A . . . some old man is staring at me, angry, he must have heard me, now there's silence . . . and the orchestra tuned up after *him*, the conductor shivered slightly, the silence is complete and in that very moment here come some late idiots, it's impossible, we have to stand up so they can pass by us, two seats are open on our left, and then the first sound spilled over us, mind-boggling, and a woman sat next to me and her sweater, a camel-hair sweater, smelled terrible, very strange, smelled of fire, no, of wood, who uses wood today, it's exactly the same smell that ceramic pot made when it broke on the stove and spilled sizzling water over the burner, but this was a long time ago, in my village, there are no wood stoves here and I don't know if that's mind-boggling, I almost didn't hear him, those two distracted me, but I'm prepared to be as mind-boggled as with the taste of my Garash cake and dry martini, he was the one who ordered the drink, and while we were waiting for it I told him a story and said—it's mind-boggling!—but it isn't mind-boggling at all, his hands are what's mind-boggling, I have to be grateful that we are sitting in the fifth row, we can hear so well and even see his hands, his face, his eyes, and most importantly that hickey of his, a welt like that really wrings your heart, he looks like he's losing his mind, really, it feels as though the violin is playing *him*, he is so natural, he is responding to it, yes, his hands are gorgeous, and they say that the violin too is something special, I saw a movie, a thriller of sorts, about a violin whose varnish was made with blood, the wife of the luthier died and he made a violin mixed with her blood, ever since then whenever I see a violin with red varnish . . . it's playing by itself, as though he isn't even there, which is an unqualified virtue, men have a hard time disappearing, they just don't have the knack for it, and I grabbed my husband's hand, because the feeling simply has to be shared, and he is contending that he doesn't know anything about music anymore, that he's been sick of everything after that competition when one of his strings broke, and to really know something about anything you need a certain verve for it, a feeling, love of some kind, I don't know, I don't trust him, I think he tends to overreact, because he is captivated by the concerto, he loves this concerto, it's his favorite Mendelssohn, he's certainly in love with the violin, he himself played the same one for a short time, almost the same, anyway, but another one of course, he was totally hypnotized, and the woman next to me who smells of fire somehow manages to shiver underneath her sweater and then smells even more strongly of fire, as if the violinist's hands boggle her mind too, mind-boggling, like the bloody violin, though this isn't the real one, probably there isn't a real one like that at all, the story was made up like most things about love, except for music, music by itself is all love, although he wouldn't agree, he has his own convictions and he well may be right, because I know nothing about music, I only listen to it alongside him, I even learned what flageolet, pizzicato, and trill mean, but I'm never entirely sure which one is which, exactly, and actually that violin in the movie was cursed, it brings bad luck, because it's been soaked with the blood of love, was it love? yes, love . . . I'm pretty sure that's how they put it, I told him while we were waiting for that dry martini, which, he said, complements the Garash cake magnificently, like a harmony in flavor, and I told him about the poll, the survey we did, and how it turned out that love only ranks *seventeenth* as far as modern priorities! *seventeenth*, can you believe it, mind-boggling, absolutely mind-boggling, I used that word and now I can't get it out of my mind—what's so mind-boggling anyway—no, I don't believe it, but things have changed so much, and then again it's not the same for men and women anyway, of course the results were an average taken from the replies of both genders, so if you look at them separately, it was actually in tenth place for women and twenty-seventh place for men, which is to the advantage of women, of course—though that probably also means to the advantage of the same men who consider love so unimportant!—well, it's mind-boggling! in about ten years love will probably have sunk to the sixty-seventh place, no, there weren't that many options on the list . . . but you know what I mean . . . and as for music . . .

it was mind-boggling, now a pause, I know I shouldn't applaud, it's not appropriate between movements, he's made that very clear to me a bunch of times, but some people don't know or can't contain their amazement and applaud, somebody is chattering behind me, philistines he said, I wanted to look back at him out of the corner of my eye, it was that old guy, and he had a callus of his own—a violinist too—and then the second movement began, second movements are always sad, slow, a bit duller, really, but otherwise pleasant, it was pleasant and tender, when you think about it music is pretty convenient, it helps you think, and it's really mind-boggling that love was in *seventeenth* place, way after money and success, even after having children . . . no, romantic love and children have nothing to do with each other, it was all so different once upon a time, but he told me—the women—yes, it used to be the first priority for women, once upon a time, with their longing, itself like music

some kind of longing

yet that man made a violin with a woman's blood, that's right, she gave birth and died, and in his sorrow he took her blood and mixed it with his varnish, that's how the violin turned red, and then he stopped his work, he didn't make any more violins, and that last violin of his became known for the bad luck it brought its owners, if you acquire the violin you die, or something like that . . . I'll ask, and anyway people taking surveys usually lie, they must be ashamed of something—*seventeenth* place it's mind-boggling, their careers are more important to them than . . . he'd finally finished, it's the end, everyone is standing up and before I know it encore, encore, encore, how mind-bogglingly fast it ended, before I even knew it, when and where did my hands start aching from all the applause . . . and he's standing next to me, he's so excited, so excited, before we came in he told me . . .

—he'll play the Chaconne for an encore,

. . . but what was that, exactly? . . .

and now he says again,

—here it is, listen to the encore, he's going to play the Chaconne . . .

and, I'll be damned, I don't remember what it means, exactly . . .

Encore!

Encore and the woman next to me stands up, she smells weird, it's not only the sweater and the wood . . . she stinks of her own longing, somehow . . .

—Mind-boggling, darling, mind-boggling . . . thank you for bringing me along, it's good that your teacher decided not to come . . . and that really seems like a terrific violin, do you remember that movie? We saw it together, about the violin—the luthier, whose wife died while giving birth, and he took her blood . . . he couldn't get over it and made a violin out of love . . .

—I remember it, it was fiction . . . and it wasn't out of love, he killed her because she was cheating on him . . . and took her blood . . .

—Well, that's still love . . . mind-boggling . . .

THE CHACONNE (THEME AND VARIATIONS)

When we recover our consciousness, the faculties may remain, if the rapture has been deep, for a day or two, and even for three days, so absorbed, or as if stunned,—so much so, as to be in appearance no longer themselves. Here comes the pain of returning to this life; here it is the wings of the soul grew, to enable it to fly so high: the weak feathers are fallen off . . . The soul now seeks not, and possesses not, any other will but that of doing our Lord's will, and so it prays Him to let it be so; it gives to Him the keys of its own will.

—Saint Teresa of Ávila,
The Life of Saint Teresa of Ávila by Herself, Chapter XX

In [the cherubim's] hands I saw a long golden spear and at the end of the iron tip I seemed to see a point of fire. With this he seemed to pierce my heart several times so that it penetrated to my entrails. When he drew it out, I thought he was drawing them out with it and he left me completely afire with a great love for God. The pain was so sharp that it made me utter several moans; and so excessive was the sweetness caused me by this intense pain that one can never wish to lose it, nor will one's soul be content with anything less than God. It is not bodily pain, but spiritual, though the body has a share in it—indeed a great share.

—Saint Teresa of Ávila,
The Life of Saint Teresa of Avila by Herself, Chapter XXIX

The moment she opened her eyes, she saw through the slightly drawn drape the curtain of snow that was descending from the sky, and had a moment to think, *you see, they predicted right, they said it would snow all day long today* before falling back asleep, after which she dreamed of snow that was coming down so heavily that it reached her windowsill, but she had to go outside nonetheless, and when she opened the door, she walked into one of those evergreen mazes at Schönbrunn, but now it was made up of tunnels chiseled out of ice . . . Again she opened her eyes.

I dreamed of Vienna.

A month ago, she'd visited Vienna to attend a competition with her best student, and who knows why, but she fell in love with the city, nostalgically, tragically, wistfully, even though she didn't like to travel, as a rule, and it'd been a while since she was enthusiastic about the place—after all, what could the city offer her that she hadn't already seen? Baroque, rococo, the Vienna Secession, our accidentally misplaced seventeenth century, gardens, fountains, and streets, streets filled with busy people . . . and the music was all still the same as ever: her ears had been desensitized after so many years of precise, critical analysis—all those notes, all those sounds, sharp and precise, driven deep into her eardrums—that it would take something truly amazing to excite them now. Such silence now, watching the falling snow. It would snow all day long. A perfect day—and there's a concert tonight . . .

I dreamed of Vienna.

But there was something about the city that had managed to disturb her, something that had managed to get past her defenses. It left her with the sense that she'd tasted, smelled, or seen something peculiar that refused to be acknowledged by her conscious mind . . . was it those spikes on the window sills, designed to stop the pigeons from perching on them and crapping on their ever so commendable cleanliness, or . . . no, not the spikes, although they're terrible things, cruel, spikes nailed in the middle of all that electrifying beauty flowing around you in triple time, of course they're horrible, but that wasn't it, and she'd seen them before anyway, no, it's something coming at her out of the corner of her eye, something simply joining in with the dance of the city and evoking a feeling of almost amorous uneasiness . . . *I must be getting old . . . it's probably menopause . . .* and she pushed away the covers cautiously, as though afraid of the cold, but it was warm in the room, the windows were a bit fogged, so that the curtain of snow outside looked as though it had been stitched together from two separate layers . . . *no, it's not menopause, it's worse . . . much worse . . .* and Vienna isn't the reason either, the reason that every morning she pushed away the covers and stretched her leg up in the air, studied her cotton pajamas, her nails, the barely visible hairs growing on her big toe, then tucked the leg and toe back under the down comforter and decided that there was no need to hurry, it was totally pointless, she could lounge around a bit more, because after all it was snowing outside, or something else was happening, something that absolutely justified said lounging and made any attempt to engage in any activity wholly unnecessary, the only necessary activity was inactivity, the sort in which you just lie there and remember your dream, and you remember Vienna, and the Schönbrunn Maze in icy colors, and you look for the cause of that unusual uneasiness, a little worm wriggling in your chest at one moment, at another in your stomach, or even somewhere in the roof of your mouth, bringing with it the taste of cake . . .—*yes, Sachertorte, that strange taste, unexpected, delicate, barely perceptible, the taste of a sentence out of Bernhard . . .*

it's so strange that I dreamed of Vienna . . . and Schönbrunn . . .

As though falling down some magnificent well . . .

No, it's not strange. What's strange is how difficult it is to admit that it's not strange.

A magnificent well, thought Virginia, and as she felt her thoughts begin to drift again, far away, far enough away that it might be difficult for them to return, this time she pushed away the down comforter with a certain decisiveness, rolled over in the big bed, and let her foot reach the ground. The thick carpet welcomed her foot; it caressed her as if to create a feeling of security, and she sat up abruptly, wrapping herself gingerly in the remaining covers to make the transition to the open air a bit easier, although the temperature in the room was nothing if not kind to her body, embracing her as though wrapping her with more feathers still, but she might have sat up too abruptly, because for a moment the bed turned into a boat gently rocking on the sea, her head was spinning and Virginia rested it in her hand, *no, not now, I won't be able to take it, if the Ménière's symptoms come back*, but the moment passed, the world became stable again along with the shapes on the carpet and now her body left the bed successfully, though this time she took things more gradually and with greater care. She went to the window and drew the curtain all the way, the rollers glided along the tracks and scratched the silence—in the blanket of white outside she saw how, moment to moment, the snow was persistently reenacting her dream—*today the earth will be covered in the colors of ice* . . . and the Schönbrunn Maze emerged from the frosted figures on the window . . .

A magnificent well, thought Virginia, again considering her dream, and for a moment it seemed to her that she was being swept through the window, that the snow playing in her eyes would simply engulf her . . . *no, not now . . . it'd kill me, I won't be able to take it* . . . and she turned her back to the window, held tight to the radiator's lukewarm ribs and half-closed her eyes, the better to shut out the persistent snow, which could make her lose her bearings, could start the world whirling around her . . . The clock in the hall behind the door started striking in the thick silence and she carefully counted the strokes—one, two, three . . .—out of simple curiosity, because she had no idea what time it was, the white blanket outside created a feeling of absolute timelessness, an endless flow and accumulation under an unvarying sky. . .

Oh my God, it's ten . . .

Certainly she needed to do something. Certainly she had missed something. Anxiety swooped down on her, it overwhelmed her like the snow and Virginia looked around, *yes, I have to remember, today is quite an ordinary day, not a Saturday, not even a Sunday, it's simply a day just like any other, the only difference being that I can't take it anymore . . .* not that it was clear what exactly she couldn't take anymore, she didn't even bother to ask herself, instead she approached the desk in the corner, taking extremely careful steps, and switched on her computer, because the glowing screen and the barely audible buzzing always made her feel connected, gave her some kind of path out of her present, toward who knew what new associations and memories, took her right to the pulse of the world, would rescue her from becoming completely lost in this one moment, veiled in the impenetrable curtain of the persistently falling snow, which she almost felt she could hear hitting the ground, despite her ears having been blocked, buried, jaded by so many sounds, so much music through the years . . . and while she was waiting for the wide world to light up on her screen, she strayed over to the piano, pressed one or two keys, stayed for a moment in their sound and even had time to contemplate it, thinking she might have to call a tuner soon, straining to catch the last hint of the notes fading away, double checking that the tuning was indeed slightly off, just slightly, and the sound seemed then to linger in the air and in her ears together with the unbearable silence outside, she reached out to touch her violin case, which was lying on an antique stand to the left of the piano—and finally the computer came to life. An Egon Schiele painting popped up on the screen, balconies and windows geometrically arranged, one over the other, with colors impossibly intensified by their recurring pattern, you might even say their rhythm, *when will I change that picture, it's depressing, I should put up the map of the Schönbrunn Maze,*

as if *that's* not depressing,

she opened a web browser, here it comes, the world is coming in, it'll force itself in, presenting itself as the ultimate opportunity, able to satisfy every whim, able to clear away this muffled, silent snow, that paints the world in the colors of ice . . .

Virginia sat at the desk and opened her e-mail, her fingers mechanically filling in her account name and password—she'd received a message just a few minutes ago . . . She knew immediately who'd sent it, without even looking, and her hand on the mouse trembled, as if it couldn't bring itself to open the letter, or was it just a tremor of anticipation in its haste to click "read," and in the seconds before the screen filled up with words, her eyes again wandered away and caught another glimpse of the snow, *how slowly it's falling . . .*

Dear Professor,

I picked up the tickets that were left for you: I collected them from the box office this morning as soon as it opened, exactly as you instructed me to do. You can't imagine how grateful I am. Without you I'd never have been able to get a ticket, to hear this Maggini—will it sound like yours?—and I really think the concert will be outstanding. While I was waiting outside the concert hall, I saw an acquaintance of mine, a musician in the orchestra, and he told me that the encore they'll perform will be the Chaconne. Can you imagine? After such a complicated program—the Chaconne. Would I ever be able to get there?

I'm very much looking forward to this evening—both to the music and to seeing you. I'll be in front of the concert hall at six forty-five precisely—is that good for you?—and remember that you should try to leave a bit earlier than usual: it's terrible outside and they say it'll continue snowing throughout the day . . . It's so white outside, and the city is so muffled, so silent . . .

In any case, I'll give you a call at twelve, between your two lessons, in case you don't get a chance to read this message in time.

And thank you once again!

M.

M.? Dear Professor? Maggini? The city is muffled? No, the Chaconne. Encore ostinato. *Exactly*—the Chaconne. More to the point, she has a class to teach in an hour, she has to make it to the Academy, has to talk to the student, to listen, to listen . . . *and I'd completely forgotten,*

dear.

What did you say? It wasn't even a thought, it was her lips that formed the word, without its first crossing her mind.

Virginia stood up and went back to the window, staring at the maze of snow flowers in the glass, growing thicker every moment—*soon I won't be able to see through, the snow will continue to pile up, perhaps the streets too will be covered with icy flowers, but I won't get to see them, not that I'd pick such a flower in any case, and I won't be able to go anywhere, I couldn't have asked for a better excuse—the cold has frozen time, it's made the hours ahead impossible to cross, it's turned them into a maze . . . and the city is dead . . . no, it's only muffled, remember . . .*

but that was just a dream.

And she still won't go anywhere—not really. She could call her students, tell them not to bother heading out into the snow, *I could do that much at least,* but no,

I won't do it, because I'm dreaming of Vienna and need to continue,

I dreamed of Vienna.

Fine snowflakes were fluttering in the air, maybe it was the first snow of the year. Sometimes it turned into rain, as if the river was melting the flakes and they could barely keep themselves in their accustomed shapes, finely scattered on the ground like salt, blown around by the incessant wind, intrusive and obstinate, which builds up in your head and causes you pain just barely on the threshold of sensitivity, pain without any pain, in exactly the same way as when her ears hurt from being too stuffed with sounds, and when she experienced that pain in an especially honest moment, she felt like screaming. Vienna was the city that she fell in love with, quite unexpectedly, and the reason wasn't St. Stephen's Cathedral with its organ, where Beethoven once . . . and before that, Bach . . . and before him, Buxtehude . . . and where, during her visit, an unknown organist almost succeeded in astounding her jaded ears, but no, it came to nothing in the end . . . And Klimt wasn't the reason either, Klimt who's even on their napkins now, a trite Klimt-reproduction smile on which she wiped her own mouth after she ate her favorite pastry, a Sachertorte, that first night in the hotel coffee shop . . . and Schiele wasn't the reason either, despite the rhythm of his balconies, which she liked so much she even put them on her computer's desktop, and when she took a special picture of the original in the Schiele hall at the Belvedere museum, she told her student—*if I look at it long enough, I will find the pattern, the rhythmic scheme, I can almost hear it, one can find the same pattern in some pieces of music too, only right now I can't think of where else to look for it, it's hiding from me . . .*—and he looked at her with astonishment, in which sentiment was also something like a silent reverence, impossible to mistake for anything else, because it was the sort of reverence one can only feel for the person who put your hand on the strings of a violin for the first time, after which you could never let go . . . and the pattern continued to be lost on her, until the following day they found themselves in front of the Schönbrunn Maze. Then she realized that what she was looking for wasn't exactly musical either, the rhythm was self-contained, in perfect harmony with the city, and she had to show it to him, to usher him in there, because it wasn't love at first sight, just the opposite, she can't even remember how many times she's already been to Vienna, but it was then that she came to understand the city for the first time, she was able to get in touch with it, and besides, in this unpleasant season of sleet, of this wind beating against your head, battering your temples, which, they say, causes depression, and a terrible urge to look for a way out of this world, it was only this last time, however, she was telling him, as she was studying the map of the maze, that she finally saw meaning in all that neurotic beauty, a beauty that drives people to hammer nails through their windowsills, to keep the pigeons off, pigeons that now leave drops of blood from their punctured bellies, when they do happen to alight . . .

. . . here is Schiele. And the Schönbrunn Maze . . . And the rhythm of the city. A drop of blood, covered in sleet, and another drop, and again sleet . . .

A magnificent well . . .

I dreamed of Vienna.

. . . There is a concert tonight.

. . . but the concert doesn't excite me. My ears are falling apart, it started right after Vienna, it started happening gradually, the wind is to blame, and it's only the Chaconne that I want to hear, I'm excited by its impossibility . . . because it's impossible to enter the maze . . .

. . . *Because it's impossible to enter the maze,* she said, *it's too cold*, it was too cold and the wind wouldn't stop screeching in her ears, and the whooshing sound got stuck in her head, between her temples, *I feel like Munch's* Scream, *you saw it, right,* but that's not the real reason, not the important reason, his hands are the real reason, because they'll freeze in this weather, they'll get numb, no gloves are thick enough, and they absolutely need to get back to the hotel right away, to warm up, and not just his hands, and then to rehearse the Chaconne again, something in it is still lost on him, *it's lost on you, I told you that much even before we headed out here, but then I didn't understand what it was, precisely, the part that you couldn't understand, but now, maybe . . .* because Vienna made it clear, she understands now, the strange love that swooped down on her like sleet, it covered her in its bittersweet coating, the taste from the Sachertorte ineradicably penetrating her palate, the taste of that piece she savored for so long in her mouth the other night in the Ritz pastry shop, where she took him only because of Bernhard's sentences, he wanted just like her to taste those sentences, and beneath the constantly moving layers in rhythmically recurring colors the drop of blood appeared, another drop of blood, and another one . . . *just like the ostinato voice*, she thought to herself, *so what's lost on me has in fact been hidden, it's somewhere deep in the structure of the piece, somewhere in its scheme, only detectable in the ostinato voice*, maybe she might even find a way to explain how it hides itself, hides in the pulsations, but she would need to find the right words, the right approach . . .

. . . but I can't seem to get it out of my head anymore, that voice which won't leave me alone . . . and I can't go to the concert either, I just won't be able to, not unless the snow stops piling up . . .

no, he won't get there either . . .

that day she saw it, a month ago, when he couldn't play the Chaconne, his palms sweating helplessly, his fingers unable to contain the music, it turned out to be bigger than him, the Chaconne, and he couldn't tame it with the sounds he was able to make, and he refused in turn to let those sounds tame him, *as if there was something shameful in it*, and instead he looked at his reflection in the eyes of the audience and of those well-dressed judges, whom, she had told him so many times, he shouldn't pay the least attention to, pretend they're not even there, they're nonexistent, *you shouldn't even look at them, you're nineteen already and you should have some basic control over yourself, when it comes to music you shouldn't think about how you look, save that for the mirror, when it's about music, it should only be about music, about that moment when the notes are driven deep into us; or, better said, when the notes drive* themselves *deep into* themselves, *the imminence and immanence they contain and imply . . .*

at the price of a drop of blood (no, she didn't say that),

for the sleet will cover it all over (and she didn't exactly say that either),

and the wind that comes after that will uncover first one later, then another one, and another still, layer by layer (and saying this would be entirely out of the question),

when . . .

when the outside world crushed him just like Medusa's eyes . . . *no, the string is absolutely not to blame,* that's what she said,

the violin is not to blame, I allowed you to play it for almost a year, ***my violin****, because that's how long it takes for one to find its anima, no matter how recalcitrant . . . even if it's a Maggini . . .*—she was so cruel after that unsuccessful performance, when it seemed as if ***her violin*** had fallen apart in his hands, she spoke to him as teacher to student, and two days before that at the Schönbrunn Maze she'd warned him—*you're losing sight of it*—but still he insisted, like a child, *let's go in, please . . .*

A magnificent well . . .

But they could come back and see the Maze some other time, when there'd be less wind . . . a day past all the sleet, out of reach of Munch's *Scream* . . .

I dreamed of Vienna.

. . . and I certainly can't go to any concert today . . . what was I thinking?

Virginia was back at her desk; she sat down for a moment and clicked "reply" . . . her hand was trembling worse than before, she felt as though her whole body was turning blurry, *I'm sorry*, she wrote, *something's come up . . . I won't be able to make it to the concert. Invite your girlfriend . . . any girlfriend . . . don't waste the ticket*—that's all she wrote, nothing more . . . *I'm pretty sure it's going to be impossible . . .* and then she sent the message, then stood up, opened the door, and went down the hallway toward the bathroom, very slowly, with all the uncertainty that her anxiety, still swelling up in her chest, gave to each of her steps . . . she felt her steps were slightly off, slightly wrong, just like that sound, invariably present in her ears for some time now, sneaking subversively around and cutting up the natural way space was apportioned here, interfering with the natural rhythms, so to speak, of space, which, as if something had suddenly taken hold of it, began warping upward along the walls and into the right angles of the ceiling, horizontally along the flat surface over which her feet moved . . . *I know what's going on, I know exactly what's happening, but I won't let it happen*, except of course that it wasn't up to her, it wasn't her decision, it was all up to the sounds themselves, the ringing in her ears, the rhythms of her body, if you try to contain them they only gush out somewhere else, driving themselves deep into the void beyond . . .

. . . Let me try again.

. . . please, dear, don't, take a break between each try.

. . . it's coming along, I'm sure of it . . .

. . . it won't, your fingers have adapted, they move too mechanically now, they slur everything, give them some time to recover . . . you shouldn't attempt the Chaconne for a few days . . .

. . . I can hear how it should sound . . .

. . . hearing it isn't enough, you should let your body do what it has to . . . give it some room to move . . . and then follow it . . .

. . . no, it doesn't work that way . . .

. . . it's the only way, you can't fake it . . .

. . . I'm sick of it . . . I'm already dreaming of Vienna . . . how much longer will I have to wait before finally going . . .

She looked at her husband, her eyes full of something, something reminiscent of disappointment, even hatred, or simply anxiety, which he could not alleviate . . . his white hair looked too white, his hand, clutching the violin, was strung with bluish veins . . .

. . . I love you, Virginia, you can do it . . .

He raised his bow and flicked back a lock of her hair that was hanging over her violin and might get tangled in one of the strings . . .

. . . it's only three more days . . . then you'll be able to do more than just dream about it . . . Then you'll have a Maggini, Virginia . . . I promise you . . .

I dreamed of Vienna.

. . . then another dream came along.

She was seeing the city then for the first time, and it

didn't meet her expectations in the least, it didn't enchant her, it wasn't at all like what she'd seen in pictures, post-cards, photo books, it wasn't what it should be, the castles were depressing with their gold ornaments, their halls lulling you with their symmetrical excessiveness, their gardens ordered in painful perfection, repelling you with their deliberate beauty; monuments sprouting at every corner: Strauss with his violin, another Strauss and then yet another, waltz time, waltz time, and more waltz time . . . then Mozart . . . *no, there isn't any Mozart here . . .*

. . . the foehn wind is to blame—

that's what he said, he knew the exact reason, just as, by the way, he knows everything, *it's the city of depression . . .* and squeezed her hand—the river had just pulled away the last patches of snow and was bringing along a barely detectable whiff of spring, while the wind subtly, if persistently, even obsessively, ate away at the façades of the houses; at the tree branches spreading out their brown fingers, still bare of any hint of the blossoms to come; at people's hair, foreheads, temples . . .

. . . the same pain without pain . . . only the season was different . . . it felt like the same wind, rising quite unexpectedly, gusting at the oddest and most inappropriate times . . .

She gave up on seeing the rest of Vienna. *I'm not interested,* she said, not even in St. Stephen's Cathedral, *I don't care to listen to any Buxtehude now,* I don't care about Mozart's house either, that seventeenth century we've absentmindedly mislaid, what does it matter where he happened to live, *he's not there anymore, he's gone, completely gone—here everything is in three-quarter time, can't you hear it?* nor was she interested in the Albertina with its dull Vienna Secession collection, *Klimt is so trite, why bother to take me there*, only Schiele remained intact in her eyes, but she could not understand his rhythm, she couldn't grasp it . . .

. . . *the foehn wind is to blame* . . . —he said

. . . *no*, she objected, *it's Munch's* Scream . . .

She locked herself up in the hotel and simply began waiting for the day, waiting for the Chaconne.

. . . *leave it be, stop trying to play it, your attitude toward the piece is absolutely unprofessional, you're just going to trample all over it . . . why not practice the other pieces, the rest of the concert will be much more important to the judges . . . why are you so obsessed . . .*

. . . And here we go, now was when she truly started dreaming of Vienna, and her real life began to insist on following the dream's lead . . .

I dreamed of Vienna.

. . . Virginia opened the bathroom door—out came an unexpected, unlikely cold, *a draft must have come in during the night, I must have left the window open last night* . . . and she stood on her tiptoes, reaching toward the small window high above the bathtub, which was gaping open . . . her palms stuck in the frost, and she hurried to push it closed—a few snowflakes swirled down slowly, her eyes following their flight . . . *Good God, look how much snow drifted in . . . it's so cold in here* . . . and then she leaned over the bathtub, looking down at where the snow had collected, as though sprouting through the white enamel . . . *here, again, the colors of ice* . . . for a long time she couldn't take her eyes off of this whiteness that had so unexpectedly accumulated in the tub, *white on white*, she kept staring at it until all the white faded into darkness and the room swam before her eyes—then she reached out and with great difficulty turned on the tap, water started trickling down, then gushed onto the sprouting snow, the stream splitting in two, in three, zigzagging down the drain, and its traces, serpentine in the snow, became a maze—she opened the tap even further, then all the way, and the hot water flooded out, melting the flowers, and the swirling waters sucked them down into the sewer, and eventually they turned back into vapor . . .

. . . *A magnificent well* . . . thought Virginia; she turned off the water and stood up, this time more abruptly than she could handle, *so I can't handle it*, and then she had no doubt about her condition, space twisted and turned around her, it stumbled sideways and then staggered back toward her, it became quite independent from her—foreign to her body—Virginia barely kept her balance, holding on to the rim of the bathtub, and a long moment passed before she could take control, stop the spinning that was dragging her and all the things around her toward a certain point, a point that lay beyond the visible, and so was free to exert the same fantastic pull on everything, radiating in every direction, vertical and horizontal, pulling at every shape and structure into which the world has grown, she managed to sit down on the cover of the toilet bowl . . . She closed her eyes. Now she just needed to wait it out . . . *yes, time is all I need*, time would eventually force space back into its proper form, somehow . . . and once that happened, all she'd need to do would be to stand up, *assuming I'll ever be able to stand up*, move slowly to the kitchen, leaning all the while against the shifting walls, make it to the medicine cabinet, open it, retrieve her pills, and then . . . in only an hour everything would be back in its place.

In only an hour everything will be all right . . .

. . . that's why I'm dreaming of Vienna . . .

. . . and nothing is in its place anymore . . .

. . . and everything used to be so simple and clear, before that man made her bleed . . .

. . . and before the Maggini . . .

. . . spelled out as if read on the palm of her hand, with no surprises, except perhaps for that prophetic unwillingness to see Vienna then, when the city still could be seen—nothing aside from Schiele and Munch—and beyond them a kind of a tiny shift, tiny and yet completely sufficient to make her believe that she was really experiencing the city some twenty years later, after she'd lived there for months—*almost twenty years later*—actually seventeen, to be precise, but precision doesn't matter save when you're talking about music, about the notes driven down deep into their destinies . . .

as he said,

there was no doubt that he was right; she had experienced it herself, and the only thing she lacked now were the words to express it—

. . . one has to be meticulous and aspire to absolute precision, to constrain oneself entirely within the bounds of an ideal fidelity, the sound is driven deep down, driven into a tone, a note, and this is already a kind of fate, the sound isn't sound anymore . . .

that man said so,

that man who made her bleed . . . most unmetaphorically.

The performance seemed to come out of nowhere, unheralded, impossible, cold, absurd, precise, and at the same time so natural. Or maybe everything had been heralding it, hidden deep down in the conventional. This was just another concert for her in Austria, after she won the competition, the last one, also in Vienna, and she was already bored with everything—she peeked at the hall from behind the curtains and saw that it was a full house, the light of the chandeliers was flickering invitingly, the orchestra was tuning its instruments and that A reaching her ears, spilling into fourth and fifth, was getting scattered into all possible nuances of sonority, usually this moment helped her concentrate and consider, but now it seemed to her that the flutes couldn't get the right sound, for some reason; she even stood on her tiptoes and looked out at them in surprise, the sound was somehow getting shifted in the wrong direction, but then the flutes quickly adjusted and she decided that maybe it was her ears that were the problem, but because of this she managed to miss the moment when the imaginary string in her had to be tightened to the right position, but there was nothing especially disturbing in that; when she stepped on stage, she had to be the one to make the definitive A, to drive it down deep into the hush of their sleeping instruments, and all of them had to copy it, and then she herself would measure the sound inside her; what was going on now was just a preliminary tuning, just in case, forcing each musician to focus on their own individual instruments . . . a moment later the light in the hall faded to complete darkness and the conductor passed by, nodded at her, smiled at her almost tenderly, and waved his hand in a show of support; she responded and considered how she barely knew the man, how except for the rehearsals she's spent almost no time with him, but it's pleasant to play with him nevertheless, he's very good, exceptionally good; he took his bow most elegantly, in fact all conductors know how to do that, it's mandatory and they don't differ when it comes to these routine gestures that are intended only to calm, to frame a space for the music, to invisibly set it aside and completely detach it from the world—her onstage gestures would be no different, any moment now, however meticulous and precise, nothing more than a fencing off of this space and time, leading to a measured focus upon the string getting tuned inside her . . . and then she performed these gestures, confident as usual, taking just a few steps, and the applause clattered through her ears, and she was holding the bow, finding the right spot on the stage . . .

. . . lifting up the bow . . .

. . . *here comes the hush* . . .

. . . the right place on stage . . . slicing precision into the sound . . .

. . . A-A-A . . .

and that A-A-A of hers resounded in the silence, terribly lonely, *it's terribly lonely*, she thought quite unexpectedly, and she was flooded by a sudden, ludicrous fear that nobody in the orchestra would play her A back to her, that the note would remain hanging in the air, wondering, just like that, in the hushed hall, in the darkness, and would rebound like a scream, *like Munch's* Scream, she thought, but, of course, this couldn't happen, didn't happen, the orchestra played her A and followed her signals quite casually, moving through their routine, moment after moment, rather ephemeral moments of the definitive tuning inside the sound, and the conductor raised his baton, raised his eyebrows in her direction, a last sign of readiness, after which all these routine movements had to finish and to be definitively conquered by the music—

but then she realized that she wasn't in her proper position after all.

It seemed to her that she was too close to the conductor's stand, too close to that baton; there it was, it could reach right out and touch her, it could lift and toss back a lock of her hair that was hanging dangerously over the strings, though there wasn't in fact a lock of hair like that, her hair was pulled tight in the back, almost like a ballet dancer's, hair fixed and safe so as not to impede the movements of her body, and Virginia stepped to the side, she moved just a bit, her eyes lowering to fix on no particular direction; she didn't respond to the conductor's raised eyebrows, although she herself quite routinely raised her violin and adjusted it as always, fitting it into that slightly hardened spot in the soft skin of her neck, automatically, out of habit, and all her eyes could see and retain at that moment was the color of the violin, a color darker than the usual, closer to the color of blood, and then the end of that baton pointing at her left temple, after which some rather peculiar thoughts began to run through her mind . . . *yes, E minor, I shouldn't forget, everything is in E*, but she couldn't possibly forget, *E minor brought her the Maggini*, this magnificent Maggini with its incredible sound, as her husband refers to it, but that she herself has earned—Virginia truly earned the violin, just as he'd promised, as if he'd known that too, *he knows everything*, and just in case she then took one more step away from the conductor's baton, just another step slightly to the side . . .

allegro molto appassionato . . .

Virginia thought finally, as if it had been a serious effort to get back to her accustomed position, to the place she was supposed to stand, and in that moment the clarinets and the bassoon entered the silence, the kettle drums bolstered them, and a note floated in the air, carried by the buzzing of the violins—one two three four—and then some latecomers caused a disturbance in the front rows—one two—but time can't wait . . . and in that moment, she let herself enter the streaming tones, her thoughts melted away as the baton continued mapping the mass of their sonorities, one note following after another, and Virginia slowly recovered her sense of time and meter . . . some part of her consciousness thought, *here everything is as it should be*; she even felt the invigorating exhalations of the audience; these were the only things she could afford to pay attention to . . . yet, without warning, another sort of awareness swooped over her, forbidden, impermissible, marginal, something to do with the nature of the space surrounding her, the nature of the space of her position on stage—and the conductor's baton went up, reached high, as if it wanted to catch her triplets, which were spilling out of her strings in an irresistible flow, but no, it wasn't the triplets that it wanted to catch, but that lock of her hair, which she knew for certain must have come loose behind her to move over her back, to tickle her gently, despite the hairpins that were rather tentatively holding it all together—that lock of her hair, that was the baton's goal . . .

Virginia, playing, took a step forward, as if her body had gotten too worked up to keep still, to keep its balance, but no, not at all . . . it was nothing less than icy anxiety, the air around her head started swirling, shutting her in and yet wandering freely through the space between the conductor's baton and the bow of her violin, which was dancing around her, following her obtrusively, hounding her, and there was no way out, now and forever she was inscribed in this self-indulgent, self-obsessed E, in which all things become nothing more than moments in time that waver unsteadily and then pass . . .

. . . and after a very brief moment her fingers succumbed to that wavering unsteadiness, or no, perhaps it was only she herself who detected the change in her playing, this momentary shift, and then in another moment her fingers had fallen back under the sway of that cold shiver that abruptly cut back through her body, and she continued to play as usual, only this time much more meticulously, precisely, methodically, she was driving the notes deep into the space around her, very clear, distinct, almost visible, certainly severe, and her eyes, usually focused inward, at the place where all the sounds came together inside her, were instead following those notes into the air, from which vantage point she could see everything—the people's faces in their seats, a kaleidoscope of expressions, eyes, hands, each reflecting her back at herself . . . and the notes. Mostly the notes in their purest forms, unvoiced, implicit . . .

. . . a drop of blood on snow, another drop and more snow . . .

. . . no, this is now, and that was before . . . but all the same . . .

. . . the foehn wind is to blame . . .

. . . it's not the foehn, it's Munch . . .

It was impossible for her to get away from the toilet seat, she had been through this before and could now feel every nuance of the shifting space around her—no, not yet. She simply needed to wait it out, to get to the point when her sensitivity would diminish and dull, when her senses would cease to register all of this information, all of this information one shouldn't even notice, let alone feel; this information one can only afford to *know*—that the Earth revolves around the sun, that the Earth is floating in nothingness and is always moving; that it's pure delusion to believe that we are each fulcra of the universe, our feet driven deep, like nails, into the ground,

even still, she could continue dreaming of Vienna, she could feel it too, all the pathways were open and Vienna could now rush into her punctured psyche, transmitted to her through the piercing ring of her cell phone, which was going off somewhere in the distance, and Virginia knew very well who was calling, but, unable to move, she couldn't find and answer it, and yet the ringing served as a sort of reference point, *so it's already twelve o'clock*—time was traveling through her so casually, but space was another story, she simply couldn't pierce it, nor could she put it back into order, space had become a labyrinth and there was no Ariadne to lead her out with red thread; even when an exit seemed to loom up in front of her, space warped around itself once more and closed it off, *I'm stuck in some simple sort of circle, a circle circling within a multitude of other simple circles . . .*

. . . they could come back and see the Maze some other time, when there'd be less wind . . . a day past all the sleet, out of reach of Munch's *Scream* . . .

The phone went silent, a few moments later she heard the ding of an arriving text message . . .

. . . impossible to pick flowers like these . . .

... there's a concert tonight, and its program is identical ... even down to the encore ... and the Maggini ...

Concert programs repeat themselves, of course; only the performances are different, better or worse. Vienna is no different—a hodgepodge of periods repeating themselves: baroque, rococo, Vienna Secession, classical, romantic, followed by our neglected seventeen century ... and now the nails driven down deep into the electric beauty of the city ... and Klimt's terribly trite kiss, you know the one, the same as any old kiss, the blandest kind imaginable, between a man and a woman, which, yes, doesn't look all that commonplace on the surface of it—one could even be fooled into thinking that it's a painting about love, really about some kind of serious passion, but no, not at all ... *that's just how it is, just how it would look if it were captured directly from life and locked into a canvas* ... and so she moved on, to avoid letting it get her down. She was fed up with the program. She'd already performed it so many times this month, always the same, almost the same, all she was allowed to change was the encore, only the encore was her choice, so she didn't even announce it beforehand for that last concert, after which she could finally rid herself of that Mendelssohn, of Vienna, that city incapable of charming her, of enchanting her,

it disenchanted her,

and mostly what she wanted to take away with her would be that fascinating Maggini, *no, it's not fascinating, it's bloody*, she thought the very first time they handed the violin to her in the storm of the applause, and she caressed it, carefully examining the lines on its body flowing into one another, the traces of its various colors, and she kissed the St. Andrew's Cross on its back, the proof that this, *only* this is a Maggini; she put her ear up to the scroll, adjusted the violin on her neck, and very slowly drew the bow across the strings . . . E, A, D, G . . . and then the first thing she played was the Chaconne, she made the decision by herself, on a whim, and then, back at the hotel, he'd called it "fascinating" . . . *its sound is fascinating, dear . . .*

. . . but no, it's actually bloody . . .

and as she said this to herself her mind conjured up the image of that piece of wood, the strung steel of its strings on top, the flexible body, its hollowness . . . *they say that somewhere in there is the anima* . . . and that night they made love—or, to be precise, he made love to her, since she kept repeating *it's bloody* to herself and she only moved mechanically, following some strange rhythm she seemed to hear coming from outside herself, like the pulse of a metronome. She didn't share this repeating thought with her husband, who certainly ended up being happier than herself, after all he had promised her and had kept his promise, which in fact she fulfilled . . . she kept her secret and he, none the wiser, left the next morning, *just business*, and she stayed on in Vienna alone, she was booked for concerts running till the end of the month, *you've always been with me when I play—one day I'll have to do it by myself . . .* but as he was leaving, while she was seeing him off, as he climbed into his cab, he didn't forgo the opportunity to give her one last piece of advice, as if maintaining the teacher-student relationship—*don't you even think of changing the program, play Beethoven and Bruch, and mostly Mendelssohn, you've perfected him, it will lead to greater things—I know, it's difficult and annoying to hear it again, but . . . and don't play the Chaconne anymore, it sounded strange last time you did it . . . you've ruined it for yourself.*

. . . the violin is to blame . . . that was the first time I used it . . .

. . . it doesn't matter, you will find its anima . . .

and he kissed her . . .

. . . she had no intention of changing anything whatsoever, had no time, had no desire, she was too busy being obsessed with her violin, *I have to find its anima*, and everything sounded different, she was slowly bonding with the violin, methodically, almost defiantly,

I have to find its anima . . .

the other thought, the strange, bloody one, only came back to her from time to time, but not obtrusively, more with a kind of coyness, even a certain revulsion, and her husband certainly turned out to be correct, because after each concert of Mendelssohn with the Maggini they overwhelmed her with flowers, whole carts full of flowers, bouquets and single flowers, bunches of flowers, flowers that would last for three whole days, others four whole days, some even lasted for a whole week, and it got to the point where she couldn't follow the process of their fading away, of their decaying, it got to the point where she couldn't separate them from each other anymore, to distinguish between them based on the fragility of their lives, and her hotel suite began sporting a perpetual smell of decay—from concert to concert, from concert to concert . . . and she could never manage to sort through them and get rid of the decaying ones . . . She tried to explain the situation to the concert organizers; she told them not to send any more flowers to her Viennese hotel, at least the flowers from her concerts out in the suburbs and countryside, *it's expensive and unnecessary*, she said, but they disagreed, and so her month-long cohabitation with those dying, semi-dead, and completely dead flowers rolled on . . .

. . . *how many icy flowers . . . and no scent . . .*

. . . at the most recent concert she even saw flowers in the audience—she saw a large yellow flower somewhere in the middle of the hall as she was beginning the andante, and while she was finagling her way through the maze of the C major, which she could barely contain—the C majors were transforming into all kinds of C minors—she found herself actively scanning the rows of seats for additional flowers, she couldn't help herself, and her eyes got caught in one after another flower muffled in the darkness of the auditorium, but were they flowers at all or simply spots of color on somebody's dress, or a shock of somebody's flaming hair, or necklaces glistening in the dark, a tiara . . . her eyes were searching, secretly, and though to look at her it might seem that those eyes were focused to the point of abstraction on her playing, Virginia was aware of the fact that she wasn't actually present, she almost couldn't hear her violin, it was being played remotely, it wasn't really under her own control, not even under its own control, and in the brief moments remaining before the allegro molto vivace she was able to think, *I have to pull myself together, I couldn't possibly finish the piece like this, it's too difficult,* and so her eyes focused on one particular white spot in the front row . . . *white isn't really a color, after all, it's all colors together, a maze of nothing . . .*

. . . *and now* . . . Virginia made a decision, positioned her legs to give herself maximum support, as though about to rise and perform a solo, then managed—just barely—to stand back up, leaning most of her weight on the nearby sink . . . *I have to take it slow, only smooth, careful motions, I have to walk without walking, no abrupt movements, no sudden twists or turns, go straight down the stairs, follow their lead, step by step, rigid as a statue above the waist . . .* keeping the most important part—the head—upright . . . inventing a surface to hold her weight, a rational solidity, indeed entirely rational, rational as opposed to actual, because she knows there's nothing there, only it's imperative that she conjures up the belief, the awareness that there's a solid support beneath and all around her and to maintain that awareness at every moment, to act as though there wasn't quicksand under her feet . . . *although that quicksand is the only reality. . .* and she did it, Virginia really stood up, driven by this will toward a rational means of moving through space, a rationality that might make bearable her terrifying sensitivity to the yielding, malleable quality of every surface with which her body might come into contact . . . here's the first step, now a second step to the slightly open door . . . she managed to grab the doorknob, she found herself stuck partway, one hand on the door—its vertical surface dragging her toward it—the other hand still clinging tightly to the sink, and as if she'd caught in a wave, hanging on for dear life, the rhythm of the world washing over her, the rhythm that makes the world flow, *no, it wasn't 3/4 time, waltz time, Vienna was in 3/4, but it wasn't 6/8 either, nothing familiar, some kind of unmeasurable pattern . . .*

. . . Schiele. Rhythmic patterns in unmeasurable flowers . . .

and yet it was indeed a pattern, so she could enter into it, or at least bluff her way through it . . . she made it out into the hallway . . . but this success didn't bring her any relief, because that's when the nausea caught up with her, *the seasickness, but I absolutely have to get to the kitchen, I have to squeeze through . . . I need to focus . . .*

. . . and then she was able to focus and finished playing her Mendelssohn, in a cold, impossible manner, so meticulously, absolutely precisely, staring quite consciously all the while at that white spot in the front row, without knowing what it actually was . . .

. . . no, it wasn't a Ménière's attack, it was something totally different: some kind of simple, clean revulsion, something left over, a trace left behind in the sound box, hiding in the violin's body right by the bridge of its sound post, the elusive anima, whereas *the Ménière's attack came along a lot later, the attack was just a symptom of that other thing, which I can't or don't want to name . . .*

. . . and when the lights came on, when she bowed—quite mechanically, with her characteristic elegance, with a smile on her face—she felt nauseated, felt as though her increasing nausea, so cold and precise, was about to spill through the crack of that smile, that meaningless smile, and she extended her bow a little too long, her eyes drilling into the floor, taking the time to pull herself together, to suppress the nausea, and she did it, she really pulled herself together, except that she wanted to run off the stage now, simply wanted to go home . . . *but it's impossible, that's not how it works, you can't run off before the sequence has been completed . . . this sequence of signs . . . these signs of the sequence . . .* and the audience is calling for their expected encore . . .

then, as soon as she righted herself, she was again able to make out the white spot in the front row, the spot that had been drawing her eyes for so long—and, in fact, it wasn't even especially white, it was a proper color after all, it was only the darkness in the hall and the black dots of the men's suits peppered all around it that had deceived her: it was a beige suit. Quite out of the ordinary, far too light a color for the stern and formal concert hall, that's why she'd seen it as white . . . *but remember, there's no such thing as white . . . white is just a maze of possible flowers . . .* The man in beige was standing up together with everyone else, but she noticed he wasn't applauding, he was looking straight at her, fixated, just as she'd been looking at him for so long without being aware of it, maybe she'd brought it on herself, but after she was able to distinguish his face, he seemed somehow familiar to her . . . *I've seen*

him somewhere before . . . and then, all of
a sudden, he cupped his hands around his mouth . . .
Virginia, or her sensitive ears, heard:

The Chaconne . . .

The Chaconne?

. . . *impossible, he told me not to play it* . . .

. . . *and now I have to* . . .

. . . *don't play the Chaconne anymore* . . .

Why do I dream of Vienna?

Because she did not, in fact, play the Chaconne. She played some Paganini, she tore through it at top speed . . . and left the stage, never suspecting that it might be the last time . . .

. . . and actually, come to think of it, there was a perfectly easy way to get to the kitchen. It was what she did the first time this happened, when the first Ménière's attack occurred; she did it instinctively, because she couldn't understand what was going on with her body and knew she had to find her way to the phone somehow, she had thought she was dying and so quite naturally dropped to the floor, started crawling, and slowly discovered that this sort of locomotion was now entirely natural to her: it was her proper mode—on all fours, her head stuck forward, crawling like a baby or like an animal, *I had the feeling I might grow a tail*, but she was only conscious of that thought later on, after her mind had returned to its normal state of equilibrium, and she'd never repeated the experiment, she only examined it within herself, the notion of her crawling, as a traumatic memory, examined it after the day the doctor told her, *there you are, already recovered, just like I said, you'll play again*, and she smiled with that same smile, the smile that didn't mean anything, because *nobody recovers from it, not that, there's no recovery once you've gone through it* . . . but she didn't say all that out loud, of course, just as she'd refrained from letting out her obsessive phrase about the drop of blood a month before,

because the snow will cover it all over (and she didn't exactly say that part either),

and then the wind after that will uncover it,

and then another layer of snow, and another gust of wind, over and again, layer by layer (and saying *that* was completely out of the question),

. . . and here the two images of Vienna merged. They faced each other and looked at themselves within each other, they saw each other and Virginia reached out for the wall, started feeling the wall, *actually what does it matter whether you're down on all fours or up on two feet* . . . since all of space is warped and the vertical axis is drooping down toward the horizontal, since the horizon is rising higher and higher and every direction can as easily be reversed, can refuse to continue along their assigned paths . . . and since nothing really matters, all that matters is getting to the kitchen, reaching the medicine cabinet, just achieving that much, taking three pills out of one small bottle, achieving that too—first one, then another one, which means two, then another one still; a fair amount, just to be certain, to be sure that her head would hold everything still again for a while, all the objects in the world, her arms and legs, and then, with her consciousness completely free of confusion, she would—precisely and meticulously, as the Chaconne should be played, *as we played the Chaconne in our hotel suite*—she'll look at one image of Vienna with one eye, and the other one with her other eye; and then her two eyes will look at themselves, look into each other, just as one image of Vienna looks into the other image of Vienna, eye into eye ... *which can only happen in the Chaconne ... or in Schiele? ... a split female body, bisected, with each part looking into the other ... one sex ... and then yet another sex ... I must be delirious ...* Virginia took a deep breath, the nausea in her chest subsided, and she started moving along the narrow hallway with her two hands outstretched—propped against the bending walls at her sides; then she reached the wide hallway, the very wide hallway, almost like a room in itself, and then her two hands were stuck to the same wall and began walking, one after the other, one next to the other, palm by palm, approaching the open door from the left, the open door through which she could see the window with its curtain fully drawn, showing the curtain of snow outside, hanging from the sky, *here it is, they predicted it correctly, they said it would snow all day long, and it keeps on snowing,* and the overabundant snow covered the earth, it had accumulated on the windowsills and was even crawling up the windowpanes in icy flowers, *of course it's not some dream, I'm simply still in that Schönbrunn Maze, evergreen, but now made out of tunnels through snow . . .*

. . . a magnificent well . . .

. . . here was the door . . .

. . . and behind it was her dressing room—she knew she should take off that expensive, open-back, performance-only dress, which enveloped her arms and shoulders so softly and tenderly, but left her back exposed so that a lock of hair could easily run down it, accidentally pulled out of the grip of the pins holding together the tight bun at the rear of her head, and could start tickling her unexpectedly, *why is the dress open in the back anyway? only the orchestra could see it,* while all their bows followed their own curved paths behind her, which she herself couldn't see . . . *why is it tailored that way?* . . . Virginia wondered and turned her back to the big dressing mirror with its two wings, reflecting her profile, she turned her head around to see herself, reached behind and felt the zipper somewhere by the middle of her spinal cord, she pulled it down and her dress fell . . . then she pulled out her hairpins, her bun uncoiled and her hair snaked down to her underwear, turning into a ponytail . . .

. . . and she heard a muffled sort of sound through the door, as if someone was scratching at it,

Virginia was startled, she ran barefoot to the wardrobe, took out her clothes, and began getting dressed—her socks, bra, blouse, skirt . . . *who could possibly be so insensitive* . . . then she went back to her dressing table, reached for her makeup remover and immediately thought better of it, her makeup wouldn't come off so easily, *I'll do it when I'm back at the hotel, I'm going there anyway,* and she could go straight back there if only she could decline the usual dinner invitation, *I'll just have to explain somehow . . .* is that why someone had knocked on her door, perhaps? to inform her that they'd be waiting for her at such and such a place, *what can I tell them . . .* in the end she put on her blazer and carefully buttoned it up . . .

. . . I've had a very bad day, please, go on without me . . .

she put on her shoes, her almost flat shoes, a relief, it's always so hard to play in heels, when any false move can make you stagger, and she felt her hands trembling a bit as she tried to do up the flat shoes' buckles and couldn't seem to maneuver their prongs through their respective holes . . .

there are still two days left before I leave . . . can't we postpone our dinner till tomorrow,

she finally managed it, stood up in front of the mirrors, stared again at her face, and in the end she left her wedding ring on her right hand, where she'd put it before the show, some people can play with a ring on their left hand, she just couldn't . . .

I've had a bad day . . .

nothing else.

She still felt, though, that there was someone out there, waiting, standing outside of her dressing-room door, she sensed someone's presence there, someone's breathing, and slowly she approached the door hoping she might catch that someone in the act, eavesdropping or peeking, she opened the door just a crack, but couldn't see anyone there . . . at the end of the hallway all she caught was a quick glimpse of the conductor and the Kapellmeister, smiling in their casual clothes, they were talking to each other, waiting for her, *it's impossible . . .* and then she closed the door again . . .

. . . I've had a really bad day, please excuse me . . .

she went back to stand in front of her mirrors, as if she couldn't tear herself away from her triple image, three separate Virginias were staring back at her, one of them from the center panel, the others from the sides, standing in the mirror's two wings, *they're so different, they say, the left and right sides of the body, it's only habit that makes us see them as a single whole, our eyes fix them one to the other* . . . she picked up her hairbrush and for no real reason brushed out her ponytail and fixed her bangs, then ran her palms along her cheeks: too much blush on them . . . *of course, this is stage makeup . . . I think I'm ready to get out of here* . . . then in the three-paneled mirror she spotted her Maggini lying on a shelf, left there somewhat carelessly, with the bow resting on top, disheveled just like herself, distressed like her, tripled like her . . . *yes, the violin, how could I forget it* . . . and she picked it up carefully, examined it; it struck her as paler here, somehow, perhaps due to the neon light, so foreign to it . . . she brushed some lint off its body with a corduroy cloth, then she held it up to her ear; she tried to peek inside it, holding the f-hole level with her eye, *somewhere inside there is a post, a bar, its anima . . . but nobody can see in there, it's too dark . . . unless it breaks open, of course . . . but then there wouldn't be any anima left to see . . .* Virginia placed the violin under her chin, squeezed it between her head and her shoulder, unusually tight, dropping her hands to her sides . . . the Maggini made a tiny cracking sound . . . *I wonder if its anima hurts . . . no, nothing can hurt it . . . it's just wood and metal . . . perfectly made . . . it only* looks *as though it's bleeding, thanks to that varnish . . .* she lifted her eyes back to the mirror and all three of her bearing their violins, and her face looked lopsided thanks to its tight grip on the instrument, her lower lips looked as though it was lolling open on one side . . . she pressed even harder with her chin, as if she wanted to hurt the instrument or hurt herself, but the violin started slipping away under the pressure, almost slipped out entirely and she had to prop it up with her left hand . . . she reached out and got the bow; she drew it slowly across the strings, tightly over the E string, and the sound it made moved rather sluggishly off into space, Virginia eased her pressure, clarified the tone, she felt how the sound box began resonating, *that's it, I'm reaching it, it's resonating . . . what else could you ask for, but earlier today it wasn't like this, not exactly . . . some coldness, a pure tone . . . must be its anima . . .* she lowered the violin and then again insistently drew to her eye again, she opened her eye wide over that narrow, impenetrable f-hole, then she squinted it nearly shut . . . *why can't the eye become an ear, no, the other way around, why can't the ear turn into an eye, to see inside everything it hears, to hear and observe . . . the anima . . .* she lost an eyelash, it drifted into her eye and it started itching and watering . . . Virginia immediately put the violin back and rubbed her eye, *my makeup will smear,* she leaned in close to one of the mirror panels and pulled down her lower lid, carefully nudging out the eyelash with her fingernail. . . *and what if my tears leaked into the body of the violin . . . into the anima . . .*

another scratch on the door startled her, although she maybe just imagined this one . . . *who could possibly . . . now of all times . . . should I just sneak away? . . . down the side hallway, through the back door . . .*

who knows why, but this thought made her smile, it made her feel good, put her at ease, she looked for the violin case . . . *it's here, it's time* . . . one of her eyes still blurry from the eyelash tear, happened to look past the window facing the yard and the parking lot, and stopped there—fell on somebody, some concert-hall employee, who she could see carefully arranging the flowers in her car, they always did that, putting them in the trunk, in the back seat, sometimes they even put flowers in the passenger seat, which meant that she couldn't avoid touching them, that her hand brushed against them whenever she changed gears, that's how she was getting back to the hotel, in that car, as if driving a hearse . . . *as though it's not enough that I have to get those flowers at all. . . meet and greet my admirers . . .*

Virginia wiped the black tearstains away with a napkin . . .

. . . I've had a very bad day . . .

she closed the Maggini case, held it tightly under

her arm, and carefully opened the dressing-room door . . .

. . . at last . . .

Virginia made it into the kitchen. She was greeted by the sight of the curtain of snow outside the window, *there's snow everywhere, icy flowers all around me, it's overwhelming, and there's a concert tonight . . . did I really think I could ever go?*

a perfect day . . . what for . . .

she stumbled toward the table, managed to catch herself, her other hand pushed the kitchen door shut behind her, and then Virginia found herself in front of a chair and sat down. She put her head in her hands to still the vibrations that her body seemed to be generating all on its own; she stayed there sitting for a while and eventually felt a bit calmer, as if the anxiety filling her chest had started to drain slowly away, to find some outlet . . . *I'm in a safe place, close to the cabinet, really close to the cabinet, one more push and I'll be there . . .* then she heard again the clock in the hallway, she hadn't even looked at it while passing by, while crawling over the wall, and its chime cut through her head now with two precise, unexpected strokes—one, two—*God, how long it took to get down here . . .* and her perfect pitch distinguished the sounds being driven deep into notes—*two beats on the kettledrums—*

E—H kettledrums,

E—H . . .

E—and that's my cue . . . how could I not have heard them before now? They're perfectly clear—

One and two and one—and here we go,

Mendelssohn resounded in her ears, it rushed into her head, *no, Mendelssohn isn't to blame, it has nothing to do with him, it's echoing in my ears specifically so that I can't hear the Chaconne, so that I won't play the Chaconne . . . I just have to move faster . . .* Virginia stood up and with unexpectedly firm steps, following the kettledrum beats in her ears, reached the cabinet at last, and in a moment the little bottle was in her hand, *this is a pause, my anxiety is draining out into this pause, but the pause can't hold it all* . . . and she counted—*one two three, let there be one more, please Mr. Mendelssohn, your triple time drives me crazy, give me another beat so my head doesn't have to spin for four more hours* . . . and the twin images of Vienna won't have to look at themselves by looking into each other, they won't have to flow through Schiele into Munch, to echo from Mendelssohn through the Chaconne . . .

. . . *only half an hour more, now . . . maybe even fifteen minutes . . . and everything will be all right . . .*

. . . *I'm going to the car, at this time of day there won't be any traffic jams, I'll be at the hotel in fifteen minutes, in twenty . . . and then I'll throw away the flowers . . .*

Virginia almost but did not begin running toward the parking lot, holding tight to the violin, the light from the Viennese streetlights elongating then foreshortening her figure, then melting it to extinction, and she carefully observed these alterations of her shadow . . . now it was growing again, the violin hanging low on her left, her double's ponytail fluttering on the other side before getting caught under somebody's shoes . . . Virginia looked up: someone was standing by her car, by his feet there were two more bouquets,

. . . not here too . . .

he approached. In the dim light her eyes eventually made out the color of his suit, beige, and she stopped a footstep away from him . . .

. . . I'm sorry, these flowers aren't from me, I know how annoying it is . . . they just couldn't fit them all in the car . . . but there are some dumpsters nearby . . . though you might need a little help hauling all of these over there . . .

She certainly needed his help. Over the next four hours the whole world was going to come to a halt, be hammered down into itself, crystal clear, purified, lucid, cold, with many hallways and corridors, easy to navigate, a maze with a rather simple design, the simplest, in which every direction leads to an entrance and every direction leads to an exit, impossible to enter, impossible to exit, the unfathomable symmetry of facing mirrors, a pattern with no sound and no color . . .

a magnificent well . . .

. . . yes, I need help . . . to throw away all these flowers . . .

She felt a desperate need for some other hand to reach out for hers.

The beige man leaned down, grabbed the two bouquets, and headed for the dumpsters; his pace was strangely confident, contained, and in the silence of the parking lot, Virginia heard his tread, which she followed with as much precise attention as she followed every note on stage; she saw him reading the cards that had come with the bouquets—she saw him consume them letter by letter, even from so great a distance, as though her own eyes had become like a cat's and could pierce the dark—he opened the right-hand dumpster, the one intended for compost, the dumpster of decay, and threw the flowers into it, but he didn't close it afterward, he came back to the car first and opened the passenger's side door, gathering up the entire pile of bouquets sitting there on the seat; in the darkness Virginia couldn't see the colors, it all looked the same to her, only the white ones stood out with their coldness—and with the same confident pace the beige man carried them away, without even asking her, *and why didn't I ever have the courage to do this?* . . . and he tossed them all away with what appeared to be a peculiar sense of satisfaction, which possibly she'd only imagined, and then he came back and this time he definitely gave her an inquisitive look—*yes, if you please, throw away the rest, I'd be grateful*, and with a smile on his face the man opened the door to the back of the car, *it's a big dumpster*, he told her, *it could take in three concert's worth* . . . and she smiled and suddenly felt calm, terribly calm . . .

her head had cleared, the world stopped spinning, calmed down completely, *the city has died . . . no, it's just been muted* . . . she could see each individual snowflake within the curtain of snow outside, *it's beautiful this way, each one of them alone, inimitably itself, made in its own image, its essence transparent . . .*

the truth is so clear . . .

—really, I've always wanted to get rid of them . . .

said Virginia when she saw the last stem sunk into the dumpster, but perhaps she didn't need to say it, because this man seemed to know it already—

—maybe you should come along with me and clean up my hotel room,

continued Virginia,

—of course I'll come. That's why I'm here . . .

that's exactly what he said.

That's why he's there, that's why Virginia was sitting there, in front of the kitchen table, fifteen minutes passed, twenty minutes passed and her eyes can focus again, the world has been pinned back into place, it's operating quite normally again, quite certain about the firmness of its various surfaces, in fact a bit too convinced, *I can stand up now, go to the telephone, make a call, get dressed, I could even go out now, go to a concert, I could do anything . . .* except that she couldn't bear this new, painful clarity, in which all the snowflakes outside seemed to be falling quite independently of one another while the sounds of the city were muffled, driven deep into the depths, she was well aware of that, she'd experienced it before, the clarity didn't give her confidence, only caused her pain, and it was terribly difficult to acknowledge the repetition—one image of Vienna in the other Vienna . . .

—no, it's not a joke, I'll do it for you, I'll do the maids' job for them, they're not gardeners after all . . . so let me come back with you, all I'd ask in return is that you play me the Chaconne . . .

the Chaconne?

The Chaconne

. . . yes, the Chaconne, because.

Later on, when, following the usual course of her illness, its rhythm, when she was going over every detail, the only thing she couldn't figure out was exactly this one point—why the Chaconne, exactly? There was some kind of connection between the Chaconne and the bloody Maggini, and it seemed that the beige man too was well aware of it, but what that connection was *exactly* she didn't grasp and he didn't care to explain. *Maggini the Chaconne Maggini the Chaconne* she kept repeating, like a mantra, even when space started warping around her for the first time and distance and direction became all jumbled up, but she still couldn't get to the bottom of the connection, still couldn't guess why *exactly* the Chaconne and no other composition. Where it came to the violin, things seemed to be a bit clearer, despite the abounding ambiguity in which it was entangled—he told her almost immediately, as they were going up in the elevator to her hotel suite, he admitted that he'd participated in that same competition, or was supposed to (and she remembered then where she had seen his face before—she had looked through the pictures of all her competitors beforehand, of course, and he was in there . . .), instead he withdrew at the last moment because he'd taken the time to investigate the violin carefully beforehand; he'd heard it and decided, no, he didn't want it—*I didn't want* ***this*** *Maggini,* he said—he had his own theory about this particular instrument, about violins in general, but it wasn't actually a theory per se, because anyone truly capable of listening could understand what he meant without any theories whatsoever, as she, Virginia, had done; she who, without ever suspecting it, had obviously been exposed to the secret—which is why he'd been so impressed with her and had followed all of her concerts, followed her ever since the competition, wherever she played her old, pre-Magginni violin (which wasn't bad, not at all, but somehow quite one-dimensional, like most ordinary violins), followed her till this very evening, when he'd finally heard her play her Maggini, because, ever since the first time he'd heard her play, he saw something in her, something in the way she touched the strings; he felt she was pre-tuned, so to speak: incredibly sensitive—she could feel every shift of her instrument's sonority and beyond, *there was no way you wouldn't be able to grasp my theory, such as it is . . .* she was a living confirmation of what he'd already known for a long time and what made him want a Maggini, *only and exactly* a Maggini, he would definitely have to have a Maggini; if it became necessary, he might even be willing to buy one himself, but *not* ***this***

one ... ***this*** Maggini was not ***his*** Maggini, *perhaps I'm just too pretentious, but ...*

Why? What's wrong with ***this one?***

... and Virginia opened the door to her hotel suite, they smelled the heavy scent of the flowers inside, fresh and decaying flowers in muddy water, *where did you get so many vases, why do you need them?* he asked, all formality gone now, interrupting his story about Magginis, as if his stepping over the threshold to her room suddenly eliminated all the world's usual conversational conventions, and Virginia shrugged her shoulders, she wasn't certain where it all came from, she just knew that everything was always covered with flowers—the table, the little shelf just below the mirror, the nightstand; they blocked the living-room windows, they covered practically every inch of floor space ... most likely the maids had been taking care of them all, giving them fresh water, trying to keep them alive, but nothing organic lasts forever, not that you could ever find the wilted ones in all of this mess ... after all, the maids weren't gardeners, after all—that's what he'd said ...

but she didn't care about that at all at this moment, she'd gotten used to the smell long ago, she only wanted to know *why*

why not my Maggini? Why not this one in particular?

... and she set down the violin on the couch by the window, looked at it with suspicion, *perhaps everything happens for a reason ... the anima ...* she even kneeled down in front of the violin, opened the case for no good reason she could think of, unsure of what she was looking for . . . she only felt alarm rushing into *her own anima* and for one short moment it was as though she had forgotten she wasn't alone — that the man with the beige suit was there, the man at whom she'd been staring for such a long time and who apparently knew something about *her* violin, something she herself didn't know and that she needed to learn — then she realized that he was standing right behind her, she could hear his breathing, and then she thought, *yes, it was him, he was the one outside my dressing-room door*, and just as quickly she chased this thought away, it was absurd . . . before she turned toward him, she felt his hand on her shoulder . . .

. . . remembering the scene later, everything that was happening seemed subsumed in the desire she felt clawing its way through her body, ignoring every barrier — and the mingled freshness and putrefaction, and the positions of the decaying flowers in their vases, turning their water clear muddy, and then a distant, faint scent of blood, sticky and neutral at the same time, spilling over from a flower of ice, suddenly wounded, dyed in red, and emanating an unexpected, insidiously odorless fragrance . . . and the Maggini, which he now reached down and took carefully out of its case, that's why he had put his hand on her shoulder, to lean over the couch and pick up the violin, maybe to show it to her, maybe to explain —

why not ***this one*** *. . . exactly?*

Virginia, still kneeling, watched —

his hands were big, but thin, his fingers too long, too soft, with protruding knuckles, too sensitive, she could tell at a glance, visibly and obviously tender, very tender, she could feel his touch as though transmitted by way of the violin—which he was now caressing—through her eyes; he embraced the body and then the elongated neck of the Maggini, two centimeters longer than that of any other violin, quite special, forcing one's fingers to bend oddly around the strings, to aspire to a feline flexibility, and if they fail, if they can't achieve it, don't find *the one and only* point at which the spaces within its sonority can be perfectly delineated and put in order, well . . .—like any violinist, she'd always notice someone's hands first and foremost: if they were delicate enough for her violin to trust them; whether or not they were flexible enough to actually play it would only be revealed at a later point, only when they actually took up the bow; these hands, however, were unusual, too big, too thick, and yet still somehow translucent—they held up the instrument securely and with confidence, caressed its body at the St. Andrew's Cross that testified that it was he, Maggini, who'd made it . . . it seemed to her that those big hands were merging with the cross, that they'd never let go of the instrument again . . . She felt something close to jealousy, got to her feet and tried to take back her Maggini, but he'd placed it under his chin, held it fast, took the bow from the case, and drew it across the strings, slowly, across all four strings, one by one, sounding a prolonged and well-defined drone, intently, with what appeared to be absolute precision,

Virginia shivered, hearing something completely unexpected—strange frequencies that seemed to reflect something outside the natural range of the resonance of the instrument's body, something that her ear really shouldn't have been able to catch, but no, those sounds were definitely coming out of the violin's bridge, without a doubt . . . yes, and this was exactly what she'd been hearing during her concert earlier—she stood watching him, astonished, heard a scream in her ears, as if the foehn had somehow sneaked into the room and pierced right through her skull—as though this wasn't the sound of ***her*** Maggini at all: the spectrum of frequencies was different, other, and yet still *the same*, the overtones driving themselves deep into the spaces of the room just like the ones that had, during the concert, turned *her* into *another*, that caused her to pass beyond her own limits, but now she was hearing it from the outside, as it were . . . was aware of that same sound being made by *his* hands . . . clean and precise and yet with a bit of vibrato, the pitch shifting quite subtly and yet palpably . . . *so the sound doesn't come from me after all, it comes from the instrument and* reveals *itself inside me . . . reveals* me . . .

one ear started listening to the other ear, both ears turned toward one another, heard the ways the other was hearing, then joined together to hear alike . . .

Maggini saw its reflection in Maggini . . .

. . . there you go . . . did you hear it? . . . only a ***Maggini*** *can challenge you like that, can dare you to make* ***it*** *come out with that sort of sound . . . would you want to play the Chaconne together?*

The Chaconne?

The Chaconne

. . . Virginia went to the wardrobe where she kept her other, her old violin. She opened the door and took out the slightly battered case, quite ordinary, that was lying on the shelf,

. . . perhaps it's lonely . . . I haven't played it even once since I got the Maggini,

she said this clearly, aloud, as though it was important to her that he hear it, and then took the case to the couch, where she opened it and removed the violin: she marveled at its smallness, its light ochre color, its bloodlessness . . . *and yet it's still precious,* Virginia said, holding it in front of her chest, as though it were a guitar, she liked to feel it touching her body, but now she had the sense that something was missing, maybe it was the absence of a St. Andrew's Cross, *but no, you can't even feel it, on the Maggini, the engraving is so light . . .* and she plucked one string with the tip of her finger . . . she felt the vibrations of its body pass into hers, the note barely making it up to her ears, where they somehow drove it away regardless; then she tried to remember what this violin sounded like, back when it was all she had, but instead of nostalgia she felt coldness, coldness in the sense of indifference, nothing like the cold flame evoked earlier this evening by the Maggini, which demanded that she take full control of its sound, never allowing her a moment's respite, and so forced her beyond her limits . . . and now she heard his voice again confirming what he'd already told her, and what she could herself feel, at that moment, through the tip of her finger, through the memory of her ear—that it wasn't a bad violin, he'd heard it many times and had evaluated it as being very good, they rarely make them so well, these days; and yet, in spite of that, it was quite one-dimensional, which isn't unusual, it was meant to be one-dimensional, or rather it *evolved* to become so one-dimensional, the common violin: time had warped the meaning of their chosen instrument, as invented by Maggini, who extracted the violin from the viola—that loving womanly instrument—and combined them, made them two in one . . . an ambivalent instrument from its very inception . . . so no, of course this violin can't be compared to a Maggini, to the transformative ability of a Maggini, *and, in the end, isn't* that *the most important quality in a violin? the ability to be everything, everywhere at once . . . after Maggini, no one dared to try to accomplish the same feat . . .*

yet, it's precious, said Virginia, with a final note of resistance in her voice, and then without a shadow of doubt remaining she admitted to herself,

yes, he's right, although it was quite comfortable, it was a part of me, my old violin . . . only missing one tiny thing . . . a big tiny thing . . . an enormous tiny thing . . .

Virginia looked into Virginia.

. . . and now how are we going to play ***together. . .***

and all of a sudden she saw everything clearly. She felt it, in fact, as though it were passing through her body: she felt it in her chest, going down to her stomach, she felt the strings taut and tuned and she felt a single crystal A note flowing along them, ready at any moment to rise or fall, to shift as much as needed, as it should when one A major parallels another, its opposite number, requiring a perfect union . . . Virginia took a step toward the beige man and raised her violin to her chin, *I'll begin, I'll set the theme . . .* but he stopped her—the Maggini was still in his hands and he offered it to her, *but of course, that's how it should be, I can't play the other one anymore . . .* Virginia saw the bow pointing at her, but the gesture wasn't threatening to her, she felt at ease in front of this man, facing her in his (relatively) bright suit, with his (actually) bright eyes, who knew *her* violin so well that Virginia herself knew it better than before, could understand it as though from inside its body, she understood now what had happened to her and knew that if she took the instrument in her hands, if she put her eye up to it, she would be able to bore into the black blanket within, penetrate into that inaccessible f-hole, see down into the dark **f** . . . *I will* ***see*** *its anima . . .*

no, she wasn't under threat at all; just the opposite . . .

she found herself wanting the bow to reach her, to flick the end of her ponytail, hanging curled up on her back, and her desire was so strong that she moved her own bow to the hand already holding her old violin and in one movement removed her hairpins with her free hand, the pins holding back her hair to make it safe for her to play, as if to give him a hint, to signal to him *do this, exactly this . . .* but instead he turned the bow around, pointing its top at himself and offering the heel to her . . .

. . . a moment ago I got the feeling that my playing your Maggini made you jealous . . . and you were right to be jealous . . .

because I'd love to play it. Of course, he wants to thank her for her gesture of confidence, their threefold harmony—instruments, music, gesture—but that's not why he came here; what he wants is to hear the Chaconne in her hands, to hear her play through that game of transformations . . . *just give me the other violin, I can handle it just fine, even if it's not completely capable of responding to me . . . anyway, I think you'd be quite bored going back to your old violin, after reaching the anima of a Maggini . . .*

you know what to do . . . right? one has to be meticulous and aspire to absolute precision, aspire to constrain oneself entirely within the bounds of an ideal fidelity; the sound is driven deep down, driven into a tone, a note, and this is already a kind of fate, the sound simply isn't sound anymore . . .

it's there that you'll find music . . .

Yes, she already knew.

She held out her old violin, and pointed the bow at him, reaching perhaps a bit too far, and farther still, as if she wanted to poke that blood-red irritation under his face, the hickey you'll find engraved on the neck of every violinist, as if she wanted to press on it and cause him pain . . . and it seemed to her that he was smiling at this impulse of hers, that he understood her . . . and so the two of them swapped violins, she took back the Maggini, embraced it, adjusted it, felt how her own red and callused flesh, into which she fitted the violin, swelled up, agitated, at its touch; as though in a mirror, she watched the beige man repeat her movement, gesture for gesture as she and he adjusted their violins with total familiarity, as she prepared to fuse with the Maggini . . .

or with ***him***?

and she raised her bow. Her first A sounded, and it looked as though he'd only barely touched his bow to the strings, his fingers had barely finished turning a tuning peg, and yet their two As merged in a perfect unison, then they split the sound into a fifth . . . and then another fifth . . .

here, it's rather precise . . . and one more fifth . . .

Virginia looked into his eyes, expecting a cue, although none was needed, she would be the one to begin . . .

. . . but it seemed to her that along with the flutter of his eyelids she also heard his voice:

The Chaconne

The Chaconne?

The Chaconne

. . . and the first chord sounded . . .

Later on, when, following the usual course of her illness, its rhythm—and it always seemed to her that this rhythm resembled nothing so much as the waves of the Chaconne—Virginia would go over every single detail of their duet that night, for as long as she could keep it in her memory and therefore put it into words that seemed to sprout from the scents of the flowers, from the smell of the marsh mud carried by the canals on rainy days, from the blood that she bled every month, or that dripped from an incidental cut on her finger . . . all details fit to share with herself alone, like the way her body felt that night, always beginning anew at her prompting, the feeling in her nerves, in her skin; what would be the point in sharing any of this with someone else, male or female? even with her doctor, who took such good care of her, tried so hard to save her after the music stopped flowing in her veins, worked to get her music pumping again, what would be the sense in talking about it? . . .

during these moments, remembering, she told herself again and again that she had to try and understand—

. . . that what I felt, what I was able to grasp in the sensation, was some exterior force telling me to go . . .

and that's where she always stopped, because she wasn't able to put it into words even for herself

how the first chord uprooted her from within herself, but with a clear head; she didn't get confused for even a moment; she knew that whatever was happening here concerned her body alone, the lower half, concerned her desire to empty herself, empty her body of her body, abandoning it, enticing her toward losing herself in sex, the perversion, the inversions that lurk somewhere at the bottom of music; and if she could only settle on a word for all this, she might choose "revelation" . . . flowing out of the Maggini's anima, out of the phrase that unfolds into the theme, out of the theme that in its unexpected transformations and mutations crawls into and inhabits her cells, out of the same triple time in which the two Viennas stare into one another, one unbearable in its dancing immediacy, the other driving the music into itself so deeply that blood drips out of its pigeons' bellies

. . . and then snow,

. . . and then again a drop, and more snow . . .

and as the rhythm of the Chaconne pulsates in an assertive andante, as the D minor is first contained and then bursts open, moving beyond itself in the ostinato voice . . . Virginia's anima was consumed by her unacknowledged revelation, consumed so naturally, organically, and at the same time so systemically, logically . . .

thus revealing that she must have assumed till then that the natural and systematic were contraries, that being engrossed by the perfection of the work would cause the natural heat of her body to wane, to cool off for the sake of her fingertips, electrified by their contact with the strings, but a painful burning became concentrated deep down in her belly as well, causing an unbearable sweetness in addition to her pain. *There's no other way forward but complete indulgence*, said Virginia, overjoyed, whispering into the dark f-holes of the violin; she didn't need to stare into them anymore because she was already in there, she'd fallen inside and was being carried away in that pitch-black sound box, where the instrument never stops vibrating.

She felt completely void of any thought, of any

involvement, and at the same time so drawn into the music—which, despite being conveyed through her fingers alone, was permeating her ears, her chest, was entering her from outside—that it frightened her; she felt a sudden, unexpected uncertainty as to whether she could resist the pressure of the music pushing her along, would she have the courage to stay where it wanted to take her, despite the pleasure . . . *the pleasure can become unbearable* . . . and despite the pain, her fingers continued to follow the music, spelling out the theme note by note, sound by sound. . .

. . . piano . . . mezzo forte . . . crescendo . . . and here it is, enter now . . .

espressivo

. . . because when she heard his violin—his, but also her own—enter the improvisation with her at the end of the theme, she briefly felt an urge to resist . . . not to resist him, certainly not the somewhat feeble sound of him playing her old violin, which could only support the Maggini, but to resist her own ecstasy, which she worried might interfere with her ability to follow the stream of eights, spilling into sixteenths, in absolute synchrony—soaring up high on the waves and then abruptly sinking down again to the lowest registers of their instruments, where the tone of her Maggini thickens and coagulates to that bloodiness before exploding in chromaticisms, following the score into the stratosphere, pulling the music up into those barely contained crystal tones, crescendo, poco crescendo, sempre crescendo . . . and her will to resist left her as abruptly as it had come, it would have been impossible to truly resist, because it's only the ecstasy that was holding together everything, that made it all possible, despite or rather due to the beige man's hands, which she practically felt on her skin—his fingers growing more and more transparent in their incredible flexibility—his eyes—following her every move—and the precision with which he matched his playing with the variable registers of her violin, keeping the rhythm pulsating from him through her in the dynamics of the impending thirty-second notes, strung along by her fingers, by his fingers in a tireless chase, one into another one over another . . .

is any of this real . . .

she might as well have wondered, but Virginia wasn't thinking anything at all, really, because her thoughts had been completely stolen by the mirage-like clarity of the sound and had traveled beyond it to where icy cold and blinding whiteness emanates from some translucent, weightless structure, concentrating itself into a ball, now on her chest, now on her belly, perhaps *exactly* in her uterus, where it was driving itself deep inside her as an acute pain one moment and burning desire the next, intervals of pleasure, intervals of silence . . . *it is painful* . . . and she wanted to liberate herself, but it was impossible, because *sweet is pleasure*, the senses can hardly resist, and Virginia closed her eyes, although even with her eyes wide open she hadn't been able to tell the dark from the light for some time now

. . . these arpeggios in pianissimo, pianissimo . . . fade away to extinction, sink deep down . . .

dolce . . . dolce . . .

. . . help me now . . .

there was only a single moment, when the triads unfolded in an endless thread, tangling up the sounds between the two of them, when she knew for certain that she'd gotten lost: she felt helpless, as if at any moment she would drop the silken thread, her only means of finding the exit, she would be swept away and then inevitably she'd fall apart—would she still be herself or would she be the music spilling down through her fingers . . . she could almost hear his voice, far away, responding to her fear—

. . . careful of the empty string . . .

and the line ended, the silk thread got drawn up into a chord, along with Virginia, and she—for the duration of a pause, a breath—sank then into limitless loneliness, mute, yearning for annihilation, death, yearning to disappear, to retreat from the world once and for all . . .

and then the sound returned . . .

it demanded her presence

poco a poco crescendo, she thought—only the musical phrases, denoting the dynamics of her body, followed by the bow, were left—he felt the dynamics of her body and Virginia heard how the accompanying violin, quite neutral till now so as not to interfere with hers, began to blossom, to swell up, and now both of them would begin to play on the G string alone, that string with the most unusual timbre, as stated explicitly in the score, because it is *required*,

sul G

the anima of her violin fused with her own, soul into soul, submerging itself in the torturous bliss of her body, which felt increasingly as though it were being elongated, pulled up, in the direction of his bow, following his wavelike movements . . .

sempre crescendo

sempre crescendo

fortissimo

and then they had to go over the whole scale again, travel through every chromatic tone, down and further down into the semitones, to a new fading away, painful, in which the tonality of the piece would change, would make its way to the major, though not yet, they're still far away,

only the expectation is tangible,

her eyes tried to open and meet his—he was looking at her, following her every flutter and now he has to let her go, to step aside, to leave it all to her . . . and the sound of his violin, which was hers, died away . . .

no, he hasn't abandoned me, it's delightful . . .

at the lowest note, the Maggini paused once more, it took a deep breath in that interval of pleasure, its sound sinking into every cranny . . . and she closed her eyes again and remained in this ecstasy, she felt as though she couldn't move ahead, she needed a bird's eye note, a fermata, that little crown, a place to release the pressure on her bow, to exhale again, but the music never stopped, it continued drawing her out of herself and she was helpless in the grip of that endless legato, intimate with even the most difficult elements of the score, the thirty-second notes followed one after another, dodging and weaving over each other, pressing against each other . . .

and then Virginia felt an incredible pain,

she saw everything being turned on its head, doubled,

Virginia stared into Virginia,

Vienna into Vienna,

Maggini into Maggini,

and everything ceased being what it was, what it is, the scent of flowers reached her nostrils, fresh flowers, semi-dead flowers, dead flowers, she took it in, she saw the man in front of her, she saw her own loneliness, she stared into him with her fingers traveling along her strings, and she wanted to amplify her abandonment of herself, to give it direction, to enter into it, into her mirror image, into her other self . . .

Virginia took a step forward, slightly off balance, repositioned her violin and entered the major . . .

Later, remembering, this moment seemed clearest to her. Maybe because she'd stopped hearing the music, by this point; the music inside her had ceased, had gone mute, had become concentrated into her fingers, solely physical, growing through her like some new organ, as the theme made itself heard in another voice entirely, that same voice she'd heard during the concert, without being able to understand what exactly it was, those nearly visible tones, absolutely precise, outwardly cold, which made her a simple appendage of her own instrument, sticking out of it like a phallus; maybe her fascination with the piece had withered at last and left her stranded in that other place, in the other, analytical part of herself . . . and two profiles flashed across her consciousness, both of herself, doubled as she saw them in the dressing room a few hours before, quite different from one another and capable of staring into each other, or maybe she was just seeing herself in the eyes of the man in front of her . . . or she had been able to penetrate the ambiguous anima of the Maggini, she awash with the impossibility of being "she," he awash in the impossibility of being "he," at the moment the music becomes completely engrossed in its own complexities and breaks through the limits of tonality . . .

here it is, let me go now, I can do it by myself, just listen, let your body listen to me . . .

and Virginia saw that he'd accepted the transformation, he'd put down both bow and violin, half-closing his eyes and accepting the soundless intervals in which the Maggini began to stretch the sound past its limits, to pull it inside out with Virginia's bow and fingers . . .

. . . now play by yourself, and start rather tenderly . . .

Virginia heard this without any words and she gathered the inexpressible dolce into her hands, dolce and again dolce, but the tone tensed up even more and rammed itself into the barely begun crescendo her fingers were getting ready for the eighths, the sixteenths, they would stop short in the abrupt strokes of the arpeggios, then in the diminuendo, which is deceptive, because the music doesn't so much abate as concentrate its power . . . until it suddenly bursts out:

sempre staccato . . . sempre staccato . . .

her fingers seemed as though they'd been sharpened, and Virginia again saw those nails driven deep into the windowsills and balcony ledges in the reversed image of Vienna.

sempre staccato

and a drop of blood,

and then snow,

and again a drop, and more snow . . .

sempre staccato

sempre staccato

sempre staccato

she felt as though she were entering a tunnel that might close up behind her, a passage leading beyond sonority taking her in and refusing to let her go, and the sound, driven into her ear, cracked into an octave, started frolicking, went as high as it could manage, the Maggini piercing deeper and deeper

al forte

fortissimo

and her hands were already feeling weak. She'd become all hands, sinking into the strings, and then the strings were sinking into her hands, and her hands felt as though they were moldering away, and the pain was stupefying . . .

. . .then the beige man raised his violin again, entered at the last restatement of the theme, fixed it in place, doubled her notes in the sort of union that can admit of no differentiation—*here we go, be me . . .*

be me . . .

sempre forte e largamente . . .

at that moment she no longer had a body. Or her whole body had fallen to pieces, and now she had to pull it back together, taking her time, and with his help—reaching the last tone, confessing . . .

confessing what . . .

. . . they both changed the direction of their bows, sawing in the opposite direction, all the way, to the very last millimeter, prolonging the note . . .

The end,

thought Virginia,

but actually it could only have been the beginning.

Virginia left her Maggini on the floor. She took the other violin from the man and left it too on the carpet.

. . . should we make love now?

his eyes, still quite bright, were locked on hers. She wanted to tell him that the last chord stays in your body forever, but it wasn't necessary, because she knew he already knew it.

. . . and will you trust me? it might be a little different from what you're used to . . .

Virginia nodded.

And later, remembering, she recalled that her hands were very cold, freezing cold after their heat had all been drawn into the strings, and how the buttons of her blouse were so difficult to get undone, and how one of them fell off and rolled toward the bow lying next to her violin.

Then she remembered her bare body stretched on the top of the suite's big double bed, and his body too, standing by her. The scent of fresh, semi-dead, and dead flowers too.

And then he took a very small knife, resembling a surgical scalpel, out of the pocket of his beige jacket . . . its sharp blade glistened in Virginia's eyes.

. . . lay down on your belly,

he told her,

and she listened to him. She had an absolute and icy trust in him.

She felt the sharpness of the blade touch her at the base of her spine—the seat of orgasm, they say . . . *how beautiful, if this is my moment to die . . .* When he slit open her skin, she didn't feel any pain. She only felt a drop of blood oozing out of the spot, leaving a narrow streak of blood, and felt how he was helping it along with his hand, channeling it or just tracing its path, as the blood reached her anus and sunk in . . .

Virginia sighed, gave herself up to his hands, which then turned her over, and she felt the blade right on the spot beneath which, inside her uterus, all her desire—articulated in her music—was concentrated. He stabbed her there lightly, painlessly, dispassionately, and more blood trickled down, flowed into her public hairs, branched out around them, gathered again in mons veneris, split into two very narrow streams that corralled her clitoris, moving around it and merging again to flow into the vagina . . .

. . . and the two streaks, the one entering via the

anus and the one entering via the vagina, met somewhere inside, and Virginia's body trembled, and then it spilled out again . . .

. . . she smelled the gentle, swampy scent of blood . . .

When she came to, she heard his voice . . .

. . . would you do the same for me? very gently . . . you have such a sure hand . . . such slender fingers . . .

***

Virginia opened her eyes. She saw another Virginia somewhere off to the side, in the dark reflections cast by the kitchen window, behind which the curtain of snow kept stretching down from the sky, piling up even higher on the windowsills, to fill in the gloom with its white glow *. . . here we go, the forecast was right, it snowed all day long, and now it's already dark* . . . and she closed her eyes again, as behind her eyelids the snow kept falling and covering the ground . . .

I dreamed of Vienna . . .

no, it's not a dream . . . everything is real . . .

she heard the clock in the hallway . . .

one

she began counting the chimes on her fingers,

how long have I been sitting here **two** *I went into the Schönbrunn Maze the next day, got lost* **three** *and I haven't even changed out of my pajamas all day, it's already dark* **four** *I overdosed on my medicine but now everything is so clear and steady* **five** *I have to turn on the lights I wonder has the concert already begun* **six** *it may have started already did I fall asleep here at the table, in the kitchen* **seven**

seven

no, no more, how many hours have I . . . did the concert already begin . . . ?

the lights in the concert hall fade.

some late couple comes in and makes the people in the front row stand up, *there's always a couple like that,*

it's already dark in the concert hall . . .

everything glistens on stage and his beige jacket glows bright in the backdrop of black tailcoats

and there are so many flowers . . . reflections, colors . . .

she unzips the dress in a single motion and it slides down . . .

I dreamed of Vienna.

In the window Virginia saw herself stand up; her hand felt for the switch, the light burst out, and behind the dark window the snow vanished, and Virginia vanished too, she melted away into the darkness, her image dissipating, submerging into the imposing silence . . . now she saw herself in the light, real, quite real, though she felt a strange torpidity in her body, which was also a readiness for what would come, which she immediately recognized, *I should have been expecting it, since he's so nearby . . . maybe he's beginning to play . . .* she left the kitchen and switched on the lamp in the hallway, looked at the huge grandfather clock to see if she had counted correctly, then she switched on the lights in the living room, then in her room, she lit up the entire house, making the snow outside seem to melt entirely away, but she knew well that in reality the storm was continuing outside, snowflake by agonizing snowflake . . .

Virginia felt the hardness of every surface, the firmness of her steps, feet slightly numb but moving with precision now, and she approached the stand where the Maggini was lying in its expensive leather case; she opened it . . . *a Ménière's attack has the strange effect of shaking up the world, mixing everything up, blurring it, but then it leaves everything so clear afterward, so defined, distinct . . . crystalline . . . and in that clarity, you don't have the right to make mistakes . . .* she picked up the violin but didn't reach for the bow, fit the instrument into its usual spot on her neck, and very carefully plucked the four strings one by one with her finger . . . the notes traveled around the room in a neutral-dispassionate pizzicato,

sul E

sul A

sul D

sul G

the orchestra is already in tune, their A has saturated the silence, traveling full circle back to itself . . .

now he'll raise the bow . . .

It's so quiet . . .

. . . Virginia headed to the bathroom together with the violin. She could hear her footsteps, could feel her body drenched in cold sweat. Before she switched on the bathroom light, she saw, for the last time, in the darkness of the small window above the tub, the curtain of snow still falling upon the world outside . . .

then the electricity buzzed to life and made her squint . . .

. . . here it is now, the light swallowed her . . .

She placed the Maggini quite carefully on the top of a white towel folded on a low table, opened the cabinet, and took out a jar full of green bathtub crystals; she set it down by the tub, then turned on the water and pulled the lever to stop up the drain . . . she stared into the water, babbling and rising, babbling and rising . . .

. . . a magnificent well . . .

thought Virginia, opened the jar, and dropped a crystal into the water: it cracked open and green tentacles crawled out in all directions; first one and then another, and another, and another dissolved into the water; now she took a handful of crystals and threw them all in, and the green concentrated into a thick ball, floated for a moment, then melted, merged with the water, which was already green, really green . . .

. . . a magnificent well . . .

Virginia took off her pajama top and stood there for a time, staring into the babbling water, which had already mostly filled the tub . . . she threw in more crystals and the green saturated with a darker green, and then she took off her pajama bottoms . . .

unzipping her dress in a single motion and it slides down . . .

naked now, she continued staring into the bathtub, while the water rose to the point that it could cover her entirely . . .

she turned it off. The water went quiet.

a magnificent well . . .

thought Virginia

it's silent . . .

She picked up the Maggini, held it against her chest, felt the St. Andrew's Cross, so gently engraved, it was touching her, she felt the coldness in its lines . . . and she stayed like that for some time, until the last tiny remaining portion of her body heat flowed out into the instrument,

here comes the coldness,

she moved the violin down, even further down, so that it rested approximately over her uterus . . .

here comes the numbness,

then she replaced the Maggini on the towel.

one has to be meticulous and aspire to absolute precision, to constrain oneself entirely within the bounds of an ideal fidelity, the sound is driven deep down into a tone, and this is already fate and the sound does not sound any more . . .

Now she was ready. Her body was cold. Virginia crossed her hands over her back, at the base of the spine, the place from which, they say, the body spills itself out, and in a while her palms felt the warm trickle, she opened her fingers around it, leaned slightly forward, made way for it . . .

she breathed in the swampy scent of blood . . .

then she moved her hands to her stomach, below it, interlocking her fingers right above the mons veneris, fixing her eyes there and seeing how the little wound, the invisible scar opened just like a mouth, letting a drop fall, followed by another; her fingers relaxed, and gave way to it . . .

what I felt, what I was able to distinguish in the feeling, was some exterior force telling me to go . . .

Virginia sighed.

She lifted a leg carefully and put it into the water, followed by the other one . . .

The red crawled into the green, and began twisting . . .

Lines making up a rhythm of polymetric colors . . .

Virginia crouched down, put one hand on each lip of the bathtub, leaving a bloody trace . . .

. . . a magnificent well . . .

thought Virginia and her body relaxed into the water . . .

CONCERTO FOR SENTENCE 4

. . . no, it can't be that way . . .

. . . it can't be that way . . . but why not? . . . everything is possible and God, look at the snow outside, I don't feel like going out into the lobby I'd rather stay here, I can't do it, of course, though everything is possible, I'm entitled, allowed . . . he played like a devil . . . and he played the devilish trills of Paganini too, deliberately . . . I have to go outside, have to make it home in that snow, it's a good thing that I live so close by, though it still seems infinitely far away at the moment . . . am I showing my age after all . . . my chest is tight with fear, here it is, I don't get it, I'm old of course but that only means I have more knowledge and experience, after all, I understand more than anyone else, and yet . . . do these kids today even have ears to hear? . . . how young they are, you don't have to put up with it at other concerts . . . but my students . . .

no . . . simply no . . .

. . . yes, hello, wonderful, of course . . .

. . . yes, the magic of sound, and you, too . . .

. . . and the touch . . .

. . . exactly, *sur la touche* . . . though he has big hands . . .

. . . that hardly matters . . .

. . . but with a Maggini . . .

acquaintances everywhere, they all say the same silly things but what else is new, nothing ever changes, and one has to make small talk if you want to make your escape, I so don't want to go out . . . in the cold . . . I'm getting old for sure, I got old a long time ago so how could it be age I'm afraid of . . . no, that's not it, so what could it be?

loneliness, yes, loneliness . . .

and look at that, look who's there . . . here he comes, of course I'd forgotten, it had slipped my mind, his wife had a Maggini, his ex . . . a real Maggini. . . we're almost neighbors . . . should I join him and walk with him, if I go over to him we'll have to have a conversation, true, but so what, we're colleagues, and everything is white outside, completely white like his hair, like my hair . . . he's gotten old too, I must look at least as old myself . . . and her name was Virginia, same as my wife, only mine died, and his left him, not quite the same thing, though yes Virginia left me too, in her way, by dying, by leaving me here to get old . . . what a coincidence, really, it's a rare name around here, though his Virginia was a lot younger than mine, that's true . . . I could walk with him through the snow and we could chat . . . there was some story a long time ago, I don't remember it exactly, everyone found it quite touching, she was his student and very good too, but that's how it is when one marries one's student, they always leave one day and my Virginia left me too, if only for her grave . . . and anyway, in his case . . . something strange happened, they say: the violin disappeared with her, and people were also saying that it just wasn't fair . . . no, it's not fair, to hide away a violin like that and only play for yourself, when you're alone . . . and perhaps too in front of your students, but even still, then it's only them who get to hear its magnificent sound, assuming it's really as magnificent as everyone says . . . idiotic . . . but he's heading to the door, he'll disappear outside, maybe I'll ask him to tell me the story . . . so much music, so many lights . . .

Maggini . . .

Virginia . . .

Virginia . . .

and now's the moment, I'll come up behind him, very causally, and snatch off my hat, no, I'll just lift it to him, there's too much snow to go bareheaded even for . . .

. . . . hello, yes, long time no see, we're neighbors actually, I live in the building right next to yours . . . our schedules must be quite different, though, so we rarely run into each other there . . . you don't teach anymore? You gave up? No, I can't, life without teaching scarcely bears thinking about, I'll probably die with violin in hand . . . and how did tonight's violin stack up for you? people can't appreciate it, but here we are, experts, you and I . . . actually do you mind walking a ways together with me? all this snow worries me, if it doesn't stop, the city will be completely erased by tomorrow, we'll all be buried alive . . . well, yes, I'm exaggerating a bit, but look, figurative speech is a perfectly acceptable means of getting one's point across, my friend, as I'm sure you . . . so you contend that Magginis are especially extraordinary? . . . no, I don't doubt, it sounds like a completely different instrument from the ordinary run of violin, I absolutely agree that there's something different about them, which perhaps stems from the length of their . . . no? you are sure? . . . their anima, you say? . . . and the wood, and the bow . . . but still, my friend, those two centimeters, they say, they really make it difficult, you have to use a different sort of fingering, is that not so? the different length of the . . . no, I'm not arguing with you, and you're quite right that not everyone risks trying a Maggini, but the harder way is always the better way, you and I know this well, it brings out hidden powers in anyone who rises to the challenge . . . what's that, you think it changes the person? no, I don't understand, not really, what exactly does it change . . . naturally, the path to the anima is a long, thorny one . . . as you say . . . but what an anima! . . . and, you know, you're absolutely right about that, it's too close to the viola, the way it sounds, altogether too close, but it's still a violin . . . a powerful instrument . . . yes, you make me smile, that's right, two in one and all that . . . that's what makes it so difficult, but that's also what makes for such a magnificent sound . . . no, no, please do go on, I'm truly intrigued, I didn't know that you had a special interest in Magginis, you studied them? please do go on, I'll be only too happy to listen, it will make our walk more pleasant, we'll overcome the snow with words . . . no, unfortunately I've never played such a violin, I've always wanted to get to touch one . . . you have had a chance? . . . I remember, of course, I remember your wife, she was an extraordinary violinist . . . and I see her in the Academy . . . she's a good teacher, her students are very successful . . . I didn't see her tonight, however, was she . . . ? . . . you don't know? . . . you two don't see each other? . . . I'm sorry, I didn't know, I didn't mean to bring it up, it just came out, I wasn't asking out of curiosity . . . no, I truly apologize, I didn't mean to mention it, my wife was also named Virginia . . . a rare name, around here, as you know, but she passed away . . . she left me quite early, she was barely forty-four . . . since then all I have is the violin, but let's get back to your Virginia, tell me more . . . otherwise we'll just be rehashing old memories, when it's the violin that is important . . .

. . . I confess, I never thought much about it, one accepts one's language as though it was a part of nature . . . of course, in Romance languages "violin" is masculine, whereas in Slavic languages it's feminine . . . but does that matter? . . . everyone accepts the violin unequivocally, and gender is a tricky thing in language . . . it's feminine in German too, come to think of it, whereas in English, of course, there isn't— . . . well, I don't mind it, it's a symptom of their imprecision, but what do you mean by that? naturally, yes, the viola has always been thought of as feminine, it just feels that way . . . and yet this transformation that you're talking about strikes me as odd, and why exactly Maggini opens up that rift . . . a chasm, you say . . . no, that's going too far, I think, it all sounds a bit mystical . . . yes, it's true, Magginis *do* sound mystical, they're so different from subsequent violins, and yet it's their prototype, so to speak, isn't it? . . . and yes, I can see that, how you could think that music itself has metaphysical origins . . . and certainly one could say it takes you out of the mundane . . . and yet . . . isn't it the player who's paramount, not the violin alone, doesn't it matter whether it's a professional or an amateur holding the bow, I mean if the player was just a dud, it wouldn't matter what sort of violin was being played, would it? . . . Still, how I envy you, knowing that you were at least able to play it . . . what, she didn't let you try? . . . you had to sneak behind her back just to hold it? . . . but, even so, surely, that would have been enough, for someone with an ear like yours, to feel all its possibilities, I've always longed for that, but I never got the chance . . . fate . . . . . .

. . . see what a nice walk we've had, it went fast, and when I was coming out of the auditorium I thought I'd never get home . . . it looked a million miles away, despite the fact that we actually live fairly close to the concert hall, and here we are almost home . . . we didn't even get to talk about the soloist, we didn't have time . . . yet his hands . . . naturally, not his hands per se, they almost don't matter, but did you notice during the encore, those trills, I thought that that must have been exactly how Paganini once played them, entirely on one string, completely unexpected then too . . . his peers figured he'd sold his soul to the devil, no? . . . oh what strange times, what strange times . . . yet don't you agree that there really is something demonic, certainly heretical in what we heard tonight? I'm speaking metaphorically, of course, as you well know, but I did want to make that clear . . . nothing classical, nothing classical in what we heard . . . classical music requires a certain fortitude with regard to the score, wouldn't you say? . . . . . . you don't agree? you don't think that's it? you think that he's quite the classical musician after all? . . . maybe . . . no, I didn't expect him to play the Chaconne, it's too long, too serious for an encore . . . yes, it's true, there's a freedom in his playing, but don't you find it a bit much? there are still rules . . . what rules? well, let's say a frame of sorts . . . no, honestly, I don't know, let's just say that when one strays too near the deep end of the pool, it can be a bit frightening . . . no? you find it divine . . . all right, it's divine, if you like . . . but what does that mean? what's waiting for us in there?

. . . we've had such a nice chat I'm not looking forward to getting back to my empty apartment, snow or no snow . . . what do you say we meet up again one of these days, just like this, over a coffee . . . yes, time flashes by, and the loneliness . . . me too, yes, I'm quite lonely . . . but if you're too busy . . . of course, it's amazing that we've never bumped into each other on the street, see, we live barely a few feet apart . . . it's strange, no? . . . good night . . . oh yes, what we heard tonight will resound in me for a long time too . . .

good night . . .

hard to find the keyhole in the dark and cold, the door is frozen stiff, and look, there's even snow in the keyhole . . . maybe I should blow inside, to melt it . . .

it resounds and resounds again . . .

craziness, the stuff he was handing me, mystical nonsense, I'd say, he's become a real maniac for the Maggini, well, so what, maybe I'm a maniac too . . . everyone is a maniac for something or other . . .

. . . the loneliness and again the loneliness . . .

. . . where are you, Virginia . . .

. . . Maggini . . .

CONCERTO FOR SENTENCE 5

. . . he didn't play the Chaconne.

so perhaps it was only an error in the program, or . . . but why announce the encore in advance, anyway? . . . it was his encore after all, his decision . . . and yet . . .

. . . he didn't play the Chaconne.

I'll tell her tomorrow . . . I'll tell her it was exceptionally good and yet not quite there, no, not quite there, in fact I don't like him, as a player . . . it felt as though he were hiding something from us . . . and he didn't play the Chaconne . . . but why didn't she show up, I don't get it . . . the person I brought along just wouldn't shut up—good grief, look how much snow there is, how are we ever going to get back now—and I always do what she says, why do I always do what she says, she told me to invite a friend and I did, but what a friend, she couldn't keep her mouth shut for a moment, killing my music . . . and now I have to see her off too . . . no, there are no cabs, we'll just have to walk, walk for a long time, the music will just fade away, not that I'll notice, since she won't shut up . . . and once, years ago, she knew him, didn't she . . . she had mentioned that, it was in Vienna . . .

Vienna . . . where I failed . . .

the invitation was from him to her, personally . . . and his violin was much the same, maybe sounded a tiny bit different, if she'd been there she would have been able to identify the exact difference, not that I couldn't hear it, but she would have been able to put a name to it . . . but this woman, honestly . . . still blabbering about a luthier and his wife's blood, what nonsense . . . if she would only shut up for a minute . . . and she's going to want me to stay the night now, she'll say how can you go anywhere in all this snow, women are always looking to get laid, that's all there is in their heads, but I'm not sure I'm interested . . . who knows, maybe I can also learn to spell things like that out, to use musical terminology like her, to grasp those minute differences, intervals . . . she told me so many things about the violin, especially about how Maggini made it out of the viola, she loves to tell that story, but when you really think about what those two and a half centimeters of additional length mean, it's horrible for the fingers, when she handed it to me for the first time and said *play it*, I got completely flustered, I didn't know how get the sound I wanted, it was completely out of tune and I was tingling all over . . . and the truth is that I had begged her for the opportunity, I'd dreamed of playing that violin, it's so beautiful and so real, more real than other violins, somehow, as I used to say, but maybe I shouldn't have opened my mouth, she told me that violins are vindictive and Magginis even more so, if you can't get a grip on its anima . . . and that's why I broke a string, I have to admit, I have to admit, hearing him play tonight, I was missing something, I can't go on fooling myself, but what is it I'm missing, for God's sake, I wouldn't have thought I lacked for anything, and perhaps

I just need to give it all up because it's either-or, there's no middle ground in music, that's just not how it works . . . I learned that from her . . . only I can't understand why she herself gave it up, I've listened to her recordings, she was absolutely terrific, really famous, in Vienna I allowed myself to ask her once and she snapped at me, saying *music is silence, the absence of sound* . . . I have no idea what she was trying to tell me, she said it just as we were entering the maze, entering it quite unintentionally, and look, this moron I've saddled myself with here wants to talk about love now, she was quoting some statistics even before the concert and wanted to know what I thought, I don't think anything, I don't care about that right now, love and statistics, absolute nonsense, sophistry, and for another thing I just couldn't understand what she was trying to tell me, couldn't understand why she turned pale when we read that the Chaconne was on the program, she told me I would never be able to play it, then she corrected herself saying we'd try it after all, but what she says always happens, it's terrible, and my feet are completely wet, my hands are freezing just like that time in Vienna and this idiot here next to me wants to rub them for me, she takes my hand and puts hers and mine into my pocket, it's not pleasant, but what can I do, girls are always longing for some kind of intimacy, and then too at the center of the maze she rubbed my hands, she drew a bath for me and spilled something green into it, an anti-stress remedy she said . . . and she stood there on the other side of the bathroom door as I got into the water . . . talking to me . . . talking about this and that . . .

important things, and then more about the violin . . . she said . . . you need to become its master, yes, don't let it be *your* master . . . I couldn't make out what she was saying, entirely . . . no, I heard it fine, I just didn't understand it, and then I got turned on . . . how idiotic, I got turned on and wanted her to be there with me in the bathtub, and something about that really scared me . . . what a fool . . . I thought, she's old . . . well, not all that old really . . . and I kept thinking about it through the night, I got turned on again, but what could I do, you're always a bit in love with your teacher, that's what they say, and it's true, art makes people especially close, you develop complicated relationships . . . and she's . . . no, not old really . . . she's even quite beautiful . . . just a lot older than me . . . what kind of love could we possibly . . . and I'm the idiot, she's just not interested in me . . . maybe that's exactly what really set me up for failure on the following day . . . exactly that . . . why . . . —look, I don't know why you keep blathering at me, why you're telling me all this useless junk, who cares about your statistics about love, what is "love" anyway, it's not like these people were experts, everybody just jabbers away, they think whatever they want and if some moron starts asking them questions, out it all spills, but what do they know . . . none of it means anything—why doesn't it mean anything?—nothing, it means absolutely nothing, it only has meaning when it swoops down on you—well yeah, it swoops down, and people still don't accept it—if they don't accept it then it just hasn't really swooped down on them yet, when it does swoop down, you accept it, it doesn't matter whether you want to or not—so that's what love is to you—that's what it is all right—all right, but I think you have to want it—why would you want it, what possible reason could you have for wanting it?—well it's magical—blah-blah-blah, a little sorrow, a little joy . . .—you're just intolerable—so don't tolerate me then . . .

I stared chatting, chatting, it's better that way, the only way to shut her up, otherwise she'll tell me about that violin movie again . . . let her talk, I can think about other things, about that really terrific moment, there was one moment in Mendelssohn that really struck me, I was wondering how he managed it, there's something just a bit *off* about that guy, I can feel it . . . something cold, icy even . . . something hidden . . . the way he held the violin was peculiar, there was something mysterious about his technique, and at that moment there really didn't seem to be a difference between the soloist and his instrument, as though one was merely the appendage of the other . . . no, they didn't exactly merge, not really, even I've felt "at one" with my instrument at times . . . no, it's something different . . . different . . .—I don't get how you can find all this snow enchanting, what's so enchanting when I'm about to freeze to death—fifteen more minutes—yeah, for you—for you too, if you want—wait a second—what—nothing, I was thinking about how that guy was playing—it was ravishing, only there was *something* off . . .—which something, what something—no, I don't know, I don't understand this sort of thing, it's more your department—I told you, not anymore, or so I thought, anyway, though now I'm not so sure . . . — come on, stop beating yourself up, it was just a competition, one broken string . . . — the string wasn't the issue, the committee doesn't take that into consideration — there will be other competitions — that's not the point — so what's the point — what was that *something*, tell me, what was that *something* — I read it in a magazine . . . — you only ever read magazines — is that bad — never mind, tell me . . . — he was somehow . . . his friend said . . . — well, so what . . . — nothing, I'm just saying . . . — I'm asking you about his performance . . . the rest doesn't matter, it doesn't matter what kind of a man he is — maybe it does matter — damn it . . . why do I even bother trying . . .

let's keep quiet for a bit, the city's never been so silent, it couldn't have been, listen, nothing, absolutely nothing is making a sound . . .

music . . .

if there are cars on the roads at all, they're barely crawling . . . nobody could clear away this endless snow and look at how it's falling in the light of the street lamps, it looks like the whole world could be swallowed up by snow . . . I wouldn't mind at all, actually I'm terribly depressed, I just can't snap out of it . . . no, it's not a passing thing, not at all, I feel worse and worse, I feel really bad and I should tell her, tell her, she'd understand, she'd give me some more of those green crystals . . . back then in Vienna they worked well . . . or maybe not so well, since it didn't exactly relax every part of me . . . I can already see her apartment building, it's tucked into the blanket of snow . . . and in the morning my eyes were a little foggy, I didn't tell her, of course, but I should have told her

darling,

did you say anything?—no, nothing—I thought you said something, spit it out—I didn't say anything, you must be hearing things—no, spit it out, you said "darling" . . . why are you so shy . . .

I don't like this cuddling, can't stand all this baby talk, "darling," honestly, as though I'd call her that, let's get a move on, hurry up, let's get there as soon as possible so I can go home, only a few more steps, only a few more notes, the string broke at the very end, absolutely horrific, but that wasn't the problem, it was the whole violin that was the problem and I had to listen to her when she told me *give up on this instrument*, but it was so beautiful, so real, and it was becoming part of me, there were moments when I felt as though it were an erection, with me waving the bow, it's an absolutely masculine instrument, the violin, there can be no doubt about that . . . all the more so for the Maggini . . . protruding, your body leaning into it, your hand moving faster and faster, but then why didn't it work, why didn't it happen? the violin and I became one, didn't we? we were completely united, I thought that I'd really gotten its anima . . . I felt . . . strong . . . and then suddenly something parted . . . parted . . . it demanded something more from me . . . something else . . . and the string simply broke, drooping down . . . and everything ended . . .

we arrived.

—are you really going to go all the way home, in this freezing cold, this blizzard . . .

. . . not really . . . no, I don't know, it's warm up there . . . so what if I go up . . . women put so much stock in getting laid . . . what do I want . . .

well . . . so what . . .

why not?

CODA

If his thigh wasn't hurting so badly, his happiness would be complete, but complete happiness doesn't exist. There will always be something in the way. The most difficult part is getting down and up the stairs, but human beings are such cunning creatures, they'll always find a way, and he has his own trick. He recites a poem, a tongue twister of sorts, in a completely unrecognizable language; the rhythm enthralls him so much that it decreases the pain and the difficulty. When he goes down the stairs, he recites it backward; when he goes up, he recites it the right way around. Just now he's going down the stairs:

Sancte Johannes
Labii reatum
Solve polluti
Famuli tuorum
Mira gestorum
Resonare fibris
Ut queant laxis

He had heard it years before from a gentleman, a musician, who was rehearsing in the concert hall; it sounded so strange to him that he asked the man to repeat it, and then repeat it again . . . he didn't explain what it meant, only saying that it was some kind of scale. He never bothered looking the words up, but he'd memorized it almost immediately, and now it was helping him in his ascending and descending:

Sancte Johannes

a stair.

Labii reatum

a stair . . . .

and he gets into the rhythm of it, although his is uneven due to his shortened leg. By the time he's descended five floors, he's so warmed up that in the main hall itself he's as spry as a little boy and nobody can tell how much pain he's in . . . the only thing he can't hide is the limping, but then limping doesn't get in the way of his work.

Solve polluti

a stair,

Famuli tuorum

a stair.

Tonight there will be a lot of work, because it's a big concert, all sold out, the auditorium is jam-packed, standing room only. He'll have to go over every spot and make sure it's clean, tidied up. He'll wait until he's the last person left, after everyone else is gone—the wardrobe assistants, the ushers, the janitors—to go over everything, the dressing rooms, the ground floor, the balconies, the bathrooms, the windows, and, in the end, he shuts off the electricity.

Darkness everywhere—and he leaves.

He locks up and nods at the security guard, everything is fine, and goes back up ut queant laxis. When they gave him the attic room and his position, earmarked for someone with disabilities, he felt extremely happy.

Later on, less so. The work is considered easy, but it takes a lot of responsibility, that's what they don't understand: to be the last to leave, to turn off the lights, to lock up . . . in addition to which, to be the bearer of all the keys . . . once an organist asked him to let him in during the night to rehearse on the hall's organ, since he didn't have one at home. The gentleman offered cash . . . but no. It's not allowed. The keys are a sacred trust. Accepting them means following the rules.

Mira gestorum

a stair

Resonare fibris

a stair

and right there at the landing comes the last part; it's all calculated in advance, as though the stairs were numbered to match his chant . . .

Ut queant laxis.

He could already hear the applause from where he was standing; he'd timed his descent well. The side entrance of the concert hall is exactly five paces from the door leading to the stairs up to his apartment. The snow is still falling and had long ago covered the skylight in his loft, so he was prepared for the worst, but no, the janitors had kept the walk clear, the five steps are possible, though he takes them very slowly, as though he might still slip . . . He enters the concert hall and nobody stops him, everyone knows him—that makes him feel good. But he doesn't speak a single word, because he has his own work to do, and it's more important than pleasantries, and by the time he gets it done, everyone else will be gone . . .

No words are needed.

The moment he steps inside, the clapping stops suddenly . . . that means an encore, just a bit more time; meanwhile, he'll check over the dressing room just in case. Not that it's his duty, but people are so careless, and he's the one responsible . . .

everything is fine, it's completely clean.

He sits at the far end of the lobby—he can see everything from there: who enters, who leaves, who goes up on the balconies, who comes down . . . and he waits. Time crawls slowly, but just in case . . .

Ut queant laxis.

. . . sometimes he dreams that he can hop up the stairs. Skip a stair, skip two stairs . . . going up, going down . . . Then he'd need to recite the little poem in a jumbled order, and so, imagining it, when he's sitting like this, in one spot, without any work, he likes to recite it to himself . . .

Mira gestorum

Labii reatum

. . . and then again

Ut queant laxis

Sancte Johannes

. . . except of course his body would never allow him to do that . . .

Sancte **J**ohannes . . .

Sancte **J**ohannes . . .

. . . And the last audience members leave. There's no one else left. The only one remaining is the soloist; once he's gone, then the real work begins. The soloist always leaves last, because of the greetings, the flowers . . . and sometimes the musicians change their clothes, too. Women for sure, men rarely. This one is a man, so he won't be long.

The door of the dressing room opens; no, he hasn't changed, he's come out in the same suit he was wearing a minute ago; an odd choice, different from the others, beige, he's a German or something like that, his violin was special, that's what people were saying in the days before the performance. A young girl comes out with him, she went in before he'd made it out of the auditorium, she's carrying his violin, the two of them are dressed almost identically. They are laughing. People are waiting for them at the front door, and there are cars waiting there too, they don't even need coats in the snow . . . But all of that isn't interesting. It's time for work to begin.

It's empty.

It's silent.

He gets going. His gait is a syncopated rhythm.

There's a strange smell in the concert hall, he loves it; in the evenings, before he comes down, he anticipates it, can't wait to breathe it in. It's not from the women's perfumes, it's the smell of the hall itself. When it's empty, the smell is even stronger.

He works his way out from the stage—first, the orchestra's chairs are carried out, the conductor's stand too, only the piano gets left behind, the organ; the wooden floor barely squeaks, and a few flower petals are lying on the ground . . . the janitors don't do their job well, and he'll collect them . . . now there's nothing left on stage.

Empty. He can turn off the stage lights.

There are only four stairs from the stage to the front row, but they're too tall for him, he can't get over them even with Ut queant laxis. Even if he recites it up to Sancte Johannes. That's why he goes around from behind and enters the auditorium through one of the back doors—walks along the seats, sometimes noticing stuff on them, under them . . . a piece of jewelry, a wallet . . . he always hands them over on the next day. But now it seems that he hears footsteps. No, it doesn't just seem. These are definitely steps. His bad leg swings rather abruptly, unexpectedly. He goes back to the foyer, yes, it's that girl, the one who was with the musician, she's come back, she heads to the dressing room.

He follows her, the girl turns around and smiles. She is pretty. Tall. Like an angel from a painting. Her hair is curly. She blurts out some words but he doesn't understand, they must have forgotten something inside. She goes in and in a moment comes out, carrying a flower in her hand. White. She smiles again; this time he tries to smile too—it's no sin to forget something in the dressing room. He's remained by the dressing-room door; in the meantime, she's stepped outside again, into the open air, weaving herself into the curtain of snow and finally sinking into it and away. Something's wrong. He opens the dressing-room door, and before he sees it, the smell overwhelms him—there's something wrong, of course, quite wrong: they left all the flowers, they didn't take them, he didn't take them, what should he do, if the wardrobe assistants had only seen them they'd have taken them away and been happy to have them, but what could he do with them, at most he could find room for a single bouquet . . . but he doesn't even need that much . . . what should he do . . . he'll think about it, of course, but while he's thinking, he can do the rest of his work, he's lost a lot of time, and he has to go up to the balconies . . . stairs again,

stairs again,

Ut queant laxis,

Resonare fibris . . .

. . . there's nothing on the first balcony. Usually the second one isn't used, but today however it was open, and that's good—he likes the second balcony. It's high up.

Mira gestorum

Famuli tuorum

Solve polluti

stairs,

stairs . . .

The auditorium looks best from here, the organ glistens even without the stage lights, when all the lights go out at the end, perhaps it stores the reflections somehow . . . rays . . . from what . . .

. . . from up here you can see immediately that there's nothing wrong, everything is in its place. He can sit in the front row of the balcony and look around from above, his eyes are healthy, only his eyes are healthy, so if anything was wrong—he'd see . . . and he's thinking about what to do with the flowers . . . that's what's wrong, that's what's bothering him; why did that guy leave behind his flowers. Everybody else takes them away . . . tomorrow somebody may tell him why the flowers were left here . . . but for the time being he can't understand . . . they shouldn't be here . . . and he's going to feel guilty about leaving them there . . . but maybe that's really the janitor's job . . . no, he can't figure it out. He can't decide. Nobody ever told him what to do if a star musician leaves behind his flowers. There are no instructions—neither regarding what to do nor who should do it. This is what comes of breaking the rules . . . he couldn't think of what to do.

No, he couldn't.

It's silent.

It's empty.

He turned off the stage lights himself. Now the whole auditorium is hushed.

It's peaceful.

No sound, and one can see everything from afar.

The seats.

The box seats, he never sits there, they're only for important people.

Tonight has to be exactly the same as every night, that's his job, but he's worried now because of the flowers. That girl took only one flower . . . why just one flower, white.

When he starts worrying, his eyes get bleary . . . they drag him toward sleep.

They feel heavy.

Droop.

He wants someone to save him.

... It seems to him for a moment that he sees that girl again, the one who was carrying the violin, and then carrying a flower, white, and who then disappeared in the snow, still white, but no, he doesn't see her, it's that angel, the angel mounted over the stage, with its curly hair ... sunk in between the flowers ...

... and what should I do with the flowers?

He's already falling asleep, he can't think of anything, he can't do anything, so it's better to leave, to shut off the power, to let everything fade behind him ...

... to lock up ...

... the keys have been entrusted ...

... he's the guardian ...

... and five paces away from the entrance ...

... and ...

Ut queant laxis

Resonare fibris

Mira gestorum

Famuli tuorum

Solve polluti

Labii reatum

Sancte Johannes,

Stairs.

Stairs.

EMILIYA DVORYANOVA is Associate Professor of Creative Writing at New Bulgarian University. Music, philosophy, and religion are the focus of her creative work. Her novel *The Virgin Mary's Earthly Gardens* (2006) received the Hristo G. Danov National Award for Literature, and was published in France in 2010 as *Les Jardins interdits*.

ELITZA KOTZEVA has worked as a news desk editor for Reuters Business Briefing, an Italian instructor at the College of Charleston, an English Composition instructor at Appalachian State University, and a freelance translator from Bulgarian, Czech, Slovak, and Italian into English.